FERN
FOLK
TALES

FERMANAGH
FOLK
TALES

DOREEN McBRIDE

The
History
Press
Ireland

First published 2015

The History Press Ireland
50 City Quay
Dublin 2
Ireland
www.thehistorypress.ie

British Library Cataloguing in Publication Data.
A catalogue record for this book is available from the British Library.

ISBN 978 1 84588 883 1

Typesetting and origination by The History Press

CONTENTS

Acknowledgements   7
Introduction   9

FERMANAGH PANTS (TALL TALES)

1. The Yanks Are Coming   12
2. Return to Tempo   15
3. The Cure of a Clever Wee Woman
   from Enniskillen   18
4. The Fish Who Went 'Fishing' in the River Sillees   21
5. How to Deal with a Plague of Rabbits   23
6. Lough MacNean's Talking Frog   24
7. 'It's a Long Way to Tipperary'
   and the Inniskilling Fusiliers   26
8. I Thought You Were the Parish Priest   28
9. Married to his Sister   30
10. The Warning   32
11. An Arresting Moment   34
12. Bags of Heat and Bags of Help   36
13. So You Want to Change Your Religion?   37
14. Paddy Irishman   38

FIRESIDE TALES

15.	Wee Meg Barnileg and the Fairies	41
16.	The Cooneen Ghost	52
17.	Lough Melvin and the River Sillees Are Cursed	56
18.	Banshees, Fairies, Witches and Other Fermanagh Folklore	59
19.	The Fermanagh Mystery Found in Killadeas Churchyard	70
20.	Huddon, Duddon and Dónal O'Leary	74
21.	The Mountain Dew (Poteen)	86
22.	The Remarkable Rocket	96
23.	The Great Famine (1845-1847)	108
24.	The Lake of the Fair Woman (Near Garrison)	118
25.	Folk Customs and Charms	120
26.	The Fiddler's Memorial, Castle Caldwell and Belleek Pottery	126
27.	The Dogs in Big Dog Forest	130
28.	The Defeat of Lough Erne's Pagan Gods	132
29.	Country Cures	138
30.	The Belleek One	153
31.	Fairs and Faking	156
32.	The Birth of the River Shannon	167
33.	Death and Funeral Customs	172
34.	Phil Purcell, the Pig Drover	178
35.	The Lady of the Lake	183
36.	Folk Tales Associated with Marble Arch Caves	185
	Glossary	187
	Bibliography	191

ACKNOWLEDGEMENTS

I think of the people I want to acknowledge with a mixture of pleasure and sadness. I am grateful for the fun I have had and sad because so many of my family members and old friends are no longer with us. I am particularly grateful to my Granny Henry and her sisters for, as my father said, 'filling my head with nonsense' and for giving me a love of storytelling. I am grateful, too, to my cousin Vernon Finlay, who is thankfully still very much alive, for his encouragement and for reading the manuscript and offering helpful comments.

Thanks are also due to John Reihill, chairman of Lisnaskea Historical Society, for his wonderful hospitality and for telling me so many tall tales, as well as the rest of the Lisnaskea Historical Society for their helpful comments and the fun I had with them when I visited. The book would not be what it is today without the help of the following. Dr Owen Dudley Edwards provided good advice. Dr Henry Glassie gave me permission to print, word for word, a story about the Great Famine told to him by Michael Boyle in 1972. The late Dr Jack Doyle, Senior Professor of English Literature at the University of South Carolina, Sumter Campus, pointed out the similarities between tall tales in County Fermanagh and those found in the Carolinas. Viki Herbert, local historian and author, answered my constant stream of questions with unremitting patience. Catherine Scott of Enniskillen Museum gave me useful information and pointed me in the right direction. Local historians Florence Chambers, Malcolm Duffy, Jack Johnston and Sam Craig were also great sources of information. I am thankful to Frances Quinn, a storyteller, for her encouragement.

Brian McMurray, Eddie Carr and the late Charlie McCourt told me about the ancient art of faking. Bernadette Layden, a storyteller, shared the story 'The Yanks are Coming' and pointed out how important tall tales are to residents in County Fermanagh where the tradition of sharing, and loving, tall tales is still alive and kicking. The staff of Enniskillen Library, especially Robena Elliott, and Frances Creighton of Lisnaskea Library provided valuable information. The Enniskillen Fusiliers Museum gave me information about the fusiliers.

Dr Denis Marnane taught me about the song, 'It's a Long, Long Way to Tipperary'. The late Pat Cassidy gave me a stick imbued with a cure for a bad leg, talked to me about folk cures, shared some good stories and told me about making poteen. The late Dr Bill Crawford sparked my interest in folklore. The late Dr Maurna Crozier gave good advice, was always ready to lend an ear and shared contacts with me. I thank the late Ernest Scott, the late Tom McDevitte and the late John Campbell for a lot of good Ulster *craic* and some great stories. Thanks must also go to the late Matt Doherty for the story about the rary. Linda Ballard must be thanked for her information, encouragement and the story about St Febor. I am grateful to the late Crawford Howard and to Liz Weir, both storytellers, for encouragement for sharing their knowledge and to Declan Forde who gave me permission to print 'The Belleek One'. Fergus Clery, Head of Design at Belleek Pottery, shared the story about the ghost that haunts Belleek Pottery and provided helpful feedback. Finally, I would like to thank Richard Watson for sharing folk tales about Marble Arch Caves.

INTRODUCTION

Fermanagh's diverse history is reflected in its folklore and folk tales and the humour of its inhabitants. Humorous stories are found throughout Ireland but they are particularly prevalent and treasured in Fermanagh, where they are referred to as 'pants' or 'tall tales'. A pant can be defined as a story with an unexpected ending, which nobody is expected to believe. I have not found such a concentration of humorous stories elsewhere and I was surprised by their strong resemblance to the tall tales I found in South Carolina, a likeness explained by history.

The Ulster-Scots dream of religious freedom was not realised in Ireland, so they left the country and took their Bibles, tools, language and stories with them. Huge numbers emigrated and became known abroad as the Scots-Irish. Most of the first settlers from Ireland left because they chose to do so. They were comparatively wealthy. Others had committed what would today be regarded as minor crimes, such as stealing. These people were tried and, if convicted, were transported to the New World. Many more left for America during and after the Great Famine (1845-1847). Once again, some were transported for disagreeing with government policies, such as the great Presbyterian Irish Nationalist, John Mitchel. Others, both Protestant and Catholic, left because of grinding poverty. These emigrants were often disease-ridden and so were unwelcome. They were met with job advertisements proclaiming 'Blacks and Irish need not apply'.

I was amazed to find many Afro-Americans boasting of Irish ancestry. When I was Storyteller in Residence on the Sumter Campus of the University of South Carolina, I met a charming Afro-American man who said, 'My name is McBride, like yours! That is my real name. I do not take my name after "slave daddy". My family remembered their real name through oral history during all the years we spent as slaves. I visited Ireland and discovered my oral history is correct. My ancestor was given what was then a light sentence for stealing linen. He was sold as a slave, first of all in Jamaica, before being passed on to South Carolina.'

Darker skin aside, that gentleman bore a striking resemblance to my husband! I later learnt there is a colony of black McBrides in Sumter, South Carolina.

I was stunned when, as a featured storyteller in the 1993 University of Rochester, NY, Storytelling Festival, I heard American storyteller Tiny Glover talk about Mark Twain and tell several stories attributed to him. I heard the same stories during my childhood. The oral history of Straid, near Ballyclare, County Antrim, claims Mark Twain's ancestors lived on Clements Hill before emigrating to America. Mark Twain's given name was Samuel Cleghorn Clements. Twain also made mention of the 'pea fairy' and I was the only one who had heard of her. My mother's best friend, who I called Auntie Sally, came from County Fermanagh and when she sat us down to shell peas she used to tell us to split the shells quickly if we wanted to catch a glimpse of the pea fairy jumping from one pod to another.

Henry Glassie did sterling work recording stories from County Fermanagh during the 1970s. These are an accurate snapshot of the time. They preserve the original dialect, complete with a key indicating when the teller laughed or smiled during the telling. I am grateful to him for permission to include a word-for-word transcription of a story he obtained from Michael Boyle about the Great Famine.

I have retold other stories collected by him, and others, in my own words, having acknowledged the source. This re-telling of a story is consistent with the oral tradition in Ireland, where storytellers believe it is the story that is important, not the teller. The teller will die; the aim is to ensure survival of the story. This is different from the situation in America, where storytellers copyright 'their' stories so no one else can tell them without facing possible legal action. In America some white people have learnt Native American stories and copyrighted them so they can no longer be told by Native Americans without the risk of court proceedings. In Ireland if somebody re-tells 'your' story you feel flattered because the story was worth passing on.

I am grateful to Dr Timothy Dudley Edwards for suggesting there could be a distinct difference between Protestant tales and those treasured by the Roman Catholic population. This is not the place to explore what would make for a fascinating academic study, but I have a distinct impression that Professor Edwards may be correct. I suspect Catholics tell more tales about priests! I did find that both sides of the community think their stories differ. Catholics have told me they think Protestants tell tales that have a more spiritual element with a greater emphasis on the supernatural than is the case in Catholic tales. But I was astonished to hear Protestants say the same thing about Catholic stories.

According to the 2011 census, four of the six Northern Irish counties have a predominantly Catholic population. Fermanagh is one of these. Both sides of the community place great emphasis on Fermanagh's culture, history, folklore and traditions. There is a determination to retain a distinct identity. Fermanagh was the only county in Northern Ireland that insisted on maintaining its old townland names when the Post Office introduced BT numbers. Eventually a compromise was reached, with townlands and BT numbers being part of each address. It is that attitude, along with the friendly, humorous character of Fermanagh's inhabitants, that has made collecting these folk tales such an interesting, enjoyable experience.

1

THE YANKS
ARE COMING

*I am indebted to Bernadette Layden, one of Fermanagh's
best-loved storytellers, for giving me this story at an
evening of storytelling in Derry/Londonderry.*

Maggie had a heart of gold and the habits of a clart. In other
words, she was always ready to do anyone a good turn but she was
a useless housewife. Her wee thatched cottage was full of clutter,
from floor to ceiling, and smelt of burnt food. As her husband Big
Brendan said, she burnt everything. She had even kept her babies
too long in her own personal oven; all of her six children were at
least ten days late.

Maggie was excited when a letter arrived from her relatives in
America. She always enjoyed hearing from them, but when she
opened this letter she had a shock.

'Oh!' gasped Maggie. 'The Yanks are coming to Ireland. They are
going on a coach tour and are spending two nights in Enniskillen.
They want to come and see us. Thon's terrible!'

'What's wrong with that?' asked Big Brendan. 'I'd have thought
ye'd be pleased. Ye'd have something to talk about for weeks. If they
come to see ye, ye'll have the neighbours eyes out on stalks listening to ye, so ye will.'

'Look at the state of this place. It's a tip. An' I'll be expected to
give them a wee bite til ate. An' ye know I can't cook.'

'Maggie dear, we've awful good neighbours. I'm sure they'll help you.'

And that's exactly what happened. The neighbours rallied round her and made her house sparkle with cleanliness.

'Well,' said Sally, who lived next door, 'that's that. Now we need to see about the grub. I'll make a trifle here in the house and the rest of ye can bring back sandwiches, cakes and tray bakes.'

Maggie watched with amazement as Sally placed pieces of sponge in the bottom of a cut-glass bowl, added a little sherry and a tin of fruit cocktail, then covered them with thick custard. As a finishing touch she decorated the top with small silver balls.

'I could do that,' Maggie thought. 'I'll have a go. It's easy. It's only fair that I make something for the Yanks too.'

Maggie made a lovely trifle and was busy admiring it when Big Brendan finished ploughing and came in through the kitchen door.

'What do you think of that?' asked Maggie, pointing proudly at the result of her efforts.

Big Brendan said it looked lovely, almost as good as Sally's. 'But,' he added, 'it doesn't have any of them wee silver balls on top.'

'You're right,' said Maggie. 'As you're going to market, would you ever bring me back some?'

'Aye, I will,' replied Big Brendan, who was a helpful soul.

He searched high and low for little silver balls and couldn't find any anywhere. Eventually he found some ball bearings in a builders' merchandise shop and thought, 'They're small. They're bigger than the ones I saw on top of Sally's trifle, but they are silver, so I'm sure they'll do.'

He took them home. Maggie was delighted and used them to decorate the top of her trifle.

The Yanks arrived the following day. The visit was a huge success. The house was admired, the supper enjoyed and everyone said the *craic* was mighty.

The next day some of the neighbours met at the well and began to gossip.

'Thon was a great night, last night,' they all agreed.

'I got great
relief when
I bent over
the fire!'

'Aye, it was,' said Sally, 'but I don't know what happened to me after it was all over. I had such cramps in my tummy. I thought I was dying.'

'That's strange,' replied another. 'I'd terrible cramps as well. They had me up all night, so they had. I hardly slept a wink, but I got such relief this morning when I took the poker and bent over the fire and poked it to get it going. The relief was tremendous, but sadly I farted and killed the cat!'

2

RETURN TO TEMPO

This is a story I got from my father, William Henry. During and after the Second World War, he spent a lot of time in Fermanagh. He worked in the insurance industry; his job was to travel around the countryside assessing Scutch Mills and giving quotations for insurance. He was always in good humour when he came back. He said the people were 'no fools'; they knew how to make a shrewd bargain and he always had a tall tale to tell. Unfortunately this is the only one I can remember. I am grateful to Florence Creighton, who works in Lisnaskea Library and is a member of Lisnaskea Historical Society, for adding the last sentence. I had forgotten it!

There was a fella from Tempo who emigrated to America. He found the States to be everything he had hoped for. As far as he could see, the land was flowing with milk, honey and opportunity. He, being a Fermanagh man, had the gift of the gab and was a hard worker. He made the most of his opportunities, built up a good business and eventually became a millionaire. Naturally he wanted to go back home and show off.

The Yank thought long and hard about how he'd impress his friends. Eventually he decided the best thing to do would be to ship his large car to Ireland, drive it across the country and finish his journey by travelling slowly up the main street of Tempo. Nobody there had a car, never mind one as big as his. It would cause a sensation.

The car landed safely on Irish soil. The Yank breathed a sigh of relief, got into it, filled it with petrol and set off. In those days the roads were poor so it was a long, hazardous journey from the port to Fermanagh and on to the village of Tempo. He drove up hills and down dales, then near the top of Brougher Mountain the car gave a splutter, a cough and conked out. It was as dead as a dodo.

The Yank got out and, with a lot of futtering and stuttering, managed to open the bonnet. He knew nothing about the innards of cars. At home he paid a chauffeur to drive him about and the chauffeur knew all there is to know. The Yank was stuck. He felt helpless and gazed in horror at the engine. He looked around for help. It was a remote area and he couldn't even see the friendly twinkling of light from a farmhouse. He was scratching his head in bewilderment, wondering what to do next, when a voice spoke to him.

'Your sparking plugs are dirty. Unscrew them, clean them, put them back and start the engine.'

The Yank was puzzled and looked all round.

There was nobody there.

He felt frightened.

Was he hearing a ghost or a fairy? He, being a practical Yank, didn't believe in such things. But maybe … maybe there were such things as ghosts and fairies? This was Ireland and strange things happen in Ireland. He'd heard that fairies sometimes steal humans. Perhaps he was going to be stolen? He was confused and terrified.

'You gomeral, you,' said the voice. 'Why can't you do what you're told?'

The Yank felt more confused than ever. He looked around but couldn't see anybody. The only living thing within view was a white horse standing near the fence beside his car.

'Oh! You're a right eejit,' said the voice. 'Why don't you just do as you're told? Look at your engine. Can't you see there're four sparking plugs sticking up and gazing you straight in the eye? You can easily unscrew them. Take them out one at a time, clean them on your handkerchief, Screw them back in, start up your engine and away you go. What have you got to lose?'

The Yank thought about the advice given. He had nothing to lose by following it, so he did as he was told, got into the car and drove off. He felt shaken by the experience. The more he thought about it, the more shaken he felt so he drove to the nearest village, stopped at Campbell's Bar and staggered in through the door.

The bartender glanced at him.

'You look as if you've seen a ghost,' he remarked.

The Yank explained what had happened.

'Was it a white horse, or a brown one, in the field?' the bartender asked.

'It was a white one,' said the Yank.

'You were lucky the white horse was out,' said the bartender. 'Thon brown one hasn't got an ounce of sense at all, at all, at all. It knows nothin' about cars.'

'That brown horse has no sense. It knows nothing about cars.'

3

THE CURE OF A CLEVER WEE WOMAN FROM ENNISKILLEN

I was told this story by an old friend, Dr David Erwin,
who's a great yarn spinner. I was surprised and delighted to
hear him tell a Fermanagh pant. David could not remember
where he first heard it. I am including it because the wee
woman in the story lived on the outskirts of Enniskillen.

Mickey Finn lived in the Short Strand area of East Belfast. Shortly after the Second World War he suffered terribly from constipation. He grew worried because his bowels didn't work for a week, then a second week passed. He was near driven to distraction by the end of the third week when his old friend, Paddy McClean, told him about a clever wee woman who lived on the outskirts of Enniskillen and had a great cure for constipation. Mickey didn't pay much attention at first because Enniskillen's a long way from the Short Strand in Belfast, but eventually he became so worried that he decided it would be wise to go and find her.

Poor Mickey felt desperate and uncomfortable so he walked all the way from Short Strand to the old UTA Station in Smithfield and caught the bus to Enniskillen. He found the clever wee woman without any trouble, knocked on her door and was invited in.

She welcomed him, sat him down by the fireside and gave him a wee cup of tea. She stared and stared at him as he drank his tea and ate a delicious bit of apple tart.

Eventually she spoke.

'I see,' she said. 'You're constipated.'

'I am,' said Mickey.

'Well,' she said, 'I think I can help ye.'

And with that she told him to follow her into the scullery. She took a bowl of a peculiar-looking liquid down from a shelf and a spoon from a drawer. She filled a bottle with liquid and looked at Mickey.

'Where did ye come from?' she asked.

'I think I can help you. Come on, on in and have a wee cup of tea in yer hand.'

'Belfast.'

She took a spoonful of liquid out of the bottle.

'And how did ye travel? By bus or by car?'

'By bus.'

The wee woman took another spoonful out of the bottle.

'And ye walked the last wee bit?'

'That's right,' replied Mickey. 'I walked.'

'Belfast,' she muttered. 'That'll take about three and a half hours on the bus.' She took another half spoonful of liquid out of the bottle and put the it back into the bowl.

'Now, tell me, where do you live in Belfast?'

'Short Strand.'

The wee woman removed half a teaspoon of liquid from the bottle.

'I guess it'll take you about half an hour to get from Smithfield to Short Strand,' she said.

'No,' said Mickey, 'I'm a fast walker, I can do it in twenty minutes.'

'Right,' said the wee woman, taking a drop out of the bottle. She looked steadily at Mickey and put three drops back.

'Now, last question: how do you fasten your trousers, with a zip or buttons?'

'I'm a button man,' replied Mickey.

The wee woman carefully took another drop out of the bottle before handing it to Mickey.

'Here, drink that,' she said, 'then get home as fast as you can. That'll cure your constipation!'

And, do you know, she was a very clever wee woman. She was only one button wrong!

4

THE FISH WHO WENT 'FISHING' IN THE RIVER SILLEES

Years ago my old friend, the late Dr Jack Doyle, Senior Professor of English Literature, Sumter Campus, University of South Carolina, told me a tall tale about a fish who went fishing in the South Carolina Swampland. Some time later I was stunned to hear the same story told in County Fermanagh. I was a guest of late Dermot Magee's family in Enniskillen at the time. I can't remember who told the story; I just remember being surprised to hear it. Evidently the story had travelled with the Irish migrants. People from Ulster emigrated and some travelled down the Appalachian Chain to the Carolinas, taking their traditions, language and stories with them. Tall tales are common among the black population in the Carolinas, many of whom intermarried with white slaves of Irish origin.

One day Seán was sitting on the bank of the River Sillees when he spotted a large pike. It was in a deep pool near a large willow tree that had branches hanging down over the water.

'Thon fish would make a great meal for me and my family,' he thought, 'so I'll just nip up to the house and grab the hault of my fishing gear and catch thon big brute.'

Seán spent the whole afternoon attempting to catch the pike. It was huge, the biggest fish he had ever seen. It would make a fine meal. He salivated at the thought.

After he had been sitting there for several hours he began to think the pike was laughing at him. It kept swimming to the surface, sticking out its head and looking at him with what he imagined was an amused look in its big fishy eyes. He was about to give up and return home when the fish surfaced, gave what he imagined to be a knowing look and swam under a branch of the willow tree that was hanging over the water. It spat something that looked like a nut out of its mouth and it fell into the water with a small splash.

The fish swam round, retrieved the nut, moved away from the branch, took careful aim and spat it in the direction of the willow tree. This time it landed on a branch hanging just a few inches above the water and stayed there. The fish remained underneath, watching and waiting. After a short period of time a squirrel appeared, saw the nut, moved towards it and picked it up. The big fish jumped out of the water, caught the squirrel and swallowed it.

Seán never attempted to catch that pike again and, for all anyone knows, it's still swimming around in the River Sillees, fishing for squirrels.

5

HOW TO DEAL WITH A PLAGUE OF RABBITS

This is one of the pants collected by
Henry Glassie and retold by me.

There was once a terrible plague that affected the whole of County Fermanagh, if not the whole of Ireland. Nobody could grow any vegetables; nobody, that is, except John Brodison.

One day somebody asked auld John how he managed to grow such beautiful cabbages and why they weren't eaten by rabbits.

'Auch!' said auld John. 'Sure one day I had a good idea. I went down to the quarry and filled my wee cart with big stones. When I got back home I put the stones all round my cabbage patch. Then I went down to Cathcart's shop and bought a pound of pepper. After that I dusted the stones with pepper.

'Now when the rabbits came til ate my cabbages the pepper gets up their noses and they start til sneeze. They can't help it, the poor wee souls. They sneeze and sneeze and sneeze and knock their brains out against the stones and now I've had no more trouble with them, so I haven't.'

LOUGH MACNEAN'S TALKING FROG

Siobhán Maguire was walking beside Lough MacNean, enjoying the fine sunny day and the gentle breeze wafting in from the lough. She smiled and waved when she saw Peter, who was rowing a cot (a type of wooden boat found in County Fermanagh) across the water. Her friend waved back. She watched until he was out of sight behind an island before continuing her walk.

Suddenly she heard a little voice calling, 'Kiss me! Kiss me! Kiss me!'

She tossed her long dark hair out of eyes and looked around. There was nobody there. She stopped walking to listen, but she heard nothing apart from the gentle rustle of the breeze through the rushes and the soft splashing of the little wavelets caressing the shore.

'There's nobody here,' she thought. 'It must be my imagination.'

'Kiss me! Kiss me! Kiss me!'

The voice sounded louder. Puzzled Siobhán looked around. Again she could see nothing so she continued to walk.

'KISS ME! KISS ME! KISS ME!' The voice was even louder this time and it was tinged with desperation, but there was still nobody in sight.

'KISS ME! KISS ME! KISS ME!' the voice yelled as something soft and slimy hit her bare ankle.

She looked down and there was the biggest, ugliest, slimiest frog she had ever seen in the whole of her life.

'If you kiss me, I'll turn into a handsome prince,' it said.

She bent down, picked it up and put it into her pocket.

'I said, if you kiss me, I'll turn into a handsome prince,' it yelled.

'Yes,' replied Siobhán, 'I know, but not many people have a talking frog!'

'Who needs a handsome prince?'

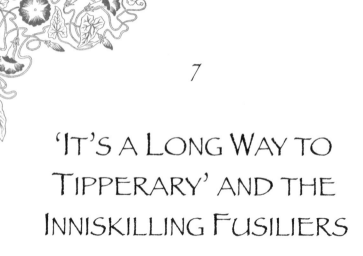

7

'IT'S A LONG WAY TO TIPPERARY' AND THE INNISKILLING FUSILIERS

*I am grateful to the Inniskilling Museum in Enniskillen
and to Dr Denis Marnane for information and
to the late Matt Doherty for the tall tale.*

The famous wartime song 'It's a long way to Tipperary' has little to do with the town of Tipperary. It began life as a music hall song written several years before the First World War by Jack Judge and Harry Williams. They wrote it in response to a five shilling bet on 13 January 1912 in Stalybridge. It was first performed the next night in the local music hall, but it didn't become popular until the beginning of the First World War, when it was picked up by the troops, who sang it as a marching song.

Tipperary had an army barracks, which recruited soldiers who signed up as infantrymen in the Inniskilling Fusiliers, based in Enniskillen.

Seán Magee signed up in the Tipperary barracks and served on the Western Front during the First World War. One day, as the battle raged, he spotted a small frightened creature crouching under a hedge. He felt sorry for it, picked it up and cuddled it. To his great surprise the animal said, 'Thank you. I feel much safer in your arms.'

'I didn't know animals could talk!' exclaimed Seán.

'Most animals can't. But I'm a rary. Raries can talk.'

'Is that so? I've never even heard of a rary.'

'That's because we're rare. You're unlikely to hear about us because there are very few of us around.'

Seán asked the rary why it was by itself, sheltering under a hedge and it told him its parents had been killed by an exploding shell. The poor little thing was all alone in the world and didn't know where to turn.

Seán felt sorry for the animal. 'I'll take care of you,' he said. He picked it up and placed it in his pocket. He grew to love it and fed it from his own rations.

Gradually other members of Seán's brigade grew to love the rary and they all fed it, which caused the other soldiers to remark, 'That creature is better fed than we are!'

Before long, the animal grew too big to fit into Seán's pocket, so he transferred it to his knapsack and carried it wherever he went. He even took it to the Battle of the Somme. The animal grew and grew and grew. It became too big to fit into a knapsack so the soldiers dressed it up in some of their old clothes and it marched alongside them.

Eventually it became so large that it was difficult to hide and it ate so much that the soldiers had difficulty feeding it. They decided the only thing to do was to kill it. Nobody could bear to put a gun to its head so one day when they were out in the mountains they decided to throw it over a cliff. That way death would be instantaneous. The rary wouldn't feel anything, there would be no mess to clean up and they would no longer be in danger of being court-martialled if the sergeant found out about its presence. They took it to the top of a high cliff and explained their predicament. The rary looked sadly over the edge of the cliff and said, 'It's a long, long way to tip a rary!'

I THOUGHT YOU WERE THE PARISH PRIEST

When I first became acquainted with the late Pat Cassidy he used to go and entertain the people in the care home for the elderly in Lisnaskea. I asked him to tell me a couple of his stories. This is one of his tall tales.

There was a young gossoon who worked for a parish priest. He looked after the priest's pony and trap and did wee jobs around the garden. The priest was strict and would not allow the lad into the house, so he slept above the pony's bed in the stable loft.

The young lad was full of fun and devilment. He loved a good ceili and sometimes sneaked out at night to have a bit of fun dancing, singing, having a wee dram and flirting with girls.

The parish priest was dead set against dancing and singing and thought any kind of fun was blasphemous, so the young lad was scared of being caught. He dreaded people falling sick in the middle of the night and sending for the priest as part of the young gossoon's job was to harness up the pony and trap and act as a driver.

One night he sneaked out and was having a great time in a ceili house when he heard that someone had taken ill. His heart leapt as he thought, 'The priest is likely to want me! I'd better get back as soon as I can. There'll be hell to pay if he finds I'm not in my bed.'

Fear lent wings to the lad's feet and he practically flew towards to the stable. He was so scared of the priest's wrath he decided to risk running past an old thorn bush growing as a short cut to the stable.

He knew fine well it was a dangerous place to be after dark. Strange things had been heard and seen around that bush. As he approached, drenched in sweat from exertion and fear, he saw a black figure waiting and watching. His knees turned to jelly and he felt as weak as holy water in an Orange Lodge. He knew if you bless yourself or speak to something that is not of this world it has the power to answer you. 'Who are you?' he quavered.

'I am the devil out of hell.'

'Thanks be to God,' he gasped. 'I thought you were the parish priest!'

'What a relief! I thought you were the parish priest.'

MARRIED TO HIS SISTER

This is another of the late Pat Cassidy's stories.

A man who lived near Belcoo had terrible rows with his wife. The pair of them were always fighting like two cats in a bag with their tails tied, except they were worse.

One night the man became so annoyed with his wife that he shot out of his house like a bullet and walked briskly towards his local pub in Belcoo. He was furious. As he walked along the road he called his wife every name under the sun, cursing and damning his soul to hell and back again as he thought of the targe he had married.

Eventually he fell into step with a stranger. He had never met the person before and yet he looked strangely familiar. The pair began to have the *craic*.

When they were passing a house, they heard a man and a woman knocking the melt out of each other and stood silently together to listen.

'I wonder what's going on in there?' asked the stranger.

'Don't ye know rightly?' replied the man. 'It's the devil outta hell in yon house.'

The stranger was terribly annoyed and knocked the man off his feet by hitting him a hefty wallop.

'What did you do that for?' asked the prone man.

'Because it's the likes of you that give me a bad name.'

'You're not the devil, are you?' asked the man.

'I am indeed.'

The man staggered to his feet, held out his hand and said, 'Put it there. I think we're related because I'm married to your sister.'

10

THE WARNING

John Reihill, who is a great storyteller and chairman of Lisnaskea Historical Society, told me this story. He knew it because his grandparents were married on the same day and in the same church in Lisknaskea as the couple in this story.

Reilly came from Derrylin. He was a big man who had a decent-sized farm and needed a wife to provide him with an heir. He eyes fell on Jane Cassidy from Lisnaskea. She was an attractive wee cutie who was so strong she could carry two buckets of water. Reilly knew that no man in his right mind would ever want a wife who'd be nothing but an ornament. The best wife was one who had a back strong enough to pull a plough and was tall enough to be able to eat hay out of a loft like a horse. Jane was just the ticket. So he set about courting her. In due course she agreed to marry him.

The pair decided to get married in the Catholic church in Lisnaskea. John suggested he take his new bride home on horse-back. She thought this was a good idea. It was a long way from Lisnaskea to Derrylin and she didn't fancy herpling along the road in her good wedding shoes.

When the big day arrived Reilly took the horse across the Erne on the ferry. (The bridge hadn't been built at the time.) The wedding went well, as did the wedding breakfast in Cassidy's Pub.

After the ceremonies were over Reilly lifted Jane up onto the horse's back and the pair headed home towards Derrylin. As they went along the road the horse stumbled. Reilly managed to catch Jane, preventing her from falling off and hurting herself. He was annoyed, glared at the horse and said firmly, 'That's once.'

They travelled on until the horse stumbled again. Reilly managed to catch Jane, settled her back on horseback and shouted, 'That's twice!'

The couple got the ferry and crossed Lough Erne without incident. When they were within a few hundred yards of home the horse caught its left hoof in a pothole and stumbled. Reilly caught Jane for the third time, set her gently on her feet, turned to the horse and said. 'That's three times! That's more than enough!'

He put his hand in his pocket, pulled out a small gun and shot the horse between the eyes.

Jane was enraged.

'What did you do that for?' she scolded. 'That was a perfectly good horse. You'd no call to kill it.'

Reilly looked at Jane, smiled and said firmly, 'That's once.'

It was a very happy marriage. Jane never argued.

AN ARRESTING
MOMENT

*This is one of John Reihill's stories.
I had great* craic *with him. Thank you, John.*

At the time of partition, Ireland was suffering from what Irish people refer to as 'troubles', so soldiers were posted in the border areas to keep watch.

Young Mark was an only child who lived near the border at Kilmore. He was known locally as a 'right young lad' who didn't drink, didn't smoke and didn't chase women. He was such a good lad his mother worried because she thought he was not long for this earth. As everyone knows, the good die young.

Mark was in his early twenties when, to his mother's delight, he started what looked like a serious friendship with Sheila, a lovely wee lass from Kilnaman.

Some mothers feel threatened when their sons start stepping out with a woman, but Mark's mother was relieved. If her worst fears were realised and he died young at least there was a chance she'd have a grandchild to love and sure, wasn't that better than being on your own?

Late one night Mark was stopped by the army when he was on his way home after he had been courting Sheila.

'Where have you come from?' demanded the soldier. He was horrified by Mark's answer, 'I've just come from Kilnaman'.

'And where are you going next?'

'I'm going to Kilmore.'

Mark had a difficult job convincing the soldier, who did not know the neighbourhood, that he had not come from killing a man and he definitely was not going to kill more!

12

BAGS OF HEAT AND BAGS OF HELP

The following stories were found in Enniskillen Library. I found the staff there, very helpful, especially Robena Elliott.

'What's it's like down there?'

Pat and Mick were reared next door to each other. They were the best of friends. They worked in the fields together, went to school together and fished together. Unfortunately one day when they were out fishing in Lower Lough Erne Mick fell in. Pat jumped in to save his friend but the weather was stormy and large waves covered the lough. Both boys drowned. Pat went to heaven and Mick went to hell.

One day Mick shouted up to Pat, 'What's it like up there?'

Pat replied, 'Heaven's not all it's cracked up to be at all, at all, at all. I'm foundered with the cold and I have to push the moon around the sky and hang the stars out at night, then take them in again in the morning. Say, how are things down there with you?'

Mick replied, 'There's bags of heat and bags of help!'

'There's bags of heat and bags of help!'

13

SO YOU WANT TO
CHANGE YOUR RELIGION?

Pat decided to make a few bob by catching the Liverpool boat and taking his pig across the water to be sold at the Liverpool market, where the prices were better than at home.

The pig grew excited and upset when Paddy drove it off the boat and into the busy streets. It was terrified by the sound of horse-drawn drays on the cobblestones and the noise of the big city on market day. It broke the straw rope Paddy had tied to one of its legs and ran like the clappers until it saw a Protestant church with the gate open. It dashed through the gate with Pat in hot pursuit.

Pat caught up with the pig and began to knock the melt out of it with his cap.

'You should be ashamed of yourself!'

'Bad cess to you!' he yelled. 'You're not in this country ten minutes and you want to change your religious faith!'

PADDY IRISHMAN

*No collection of Fermanagh tall tales would be
complete without a few about Paddy Irishman.*

SENTENCED TO BE HANGED

Paddy Irishman, Paddy Englishman and Paddy Scotsman joined
forces to steal goods during Fair Day at Belleek. Unfortunately
they were caught, put on trial and sentenced to death. For some
unknown reason, the judge decided to allow each of them to
choose the type of tree from which they would be hanged.

'If it please
your honour,
I choose to
be hung from
a gooseberry
bush.'

Paddy Englishman said, 'I choose to be hanged from a fine old English oak.' Paddy Scotsman said, 'I choose to be hanged from a fine Scots pine.' Paddy Irishman said, 'I choose to be hanged from a gooseberry bush.'

The judge looked puzzled.

'Don't you realise,' he asked, 'that a gooseberry bush is not strong enough, or tall enough, to hang you?'

Paddy replied, 'Your honour, I'm willing to wait until it grows!'

THE FLEA'S WAKE

Paddy went to England for the first time. He was very worried because he'd heard the rooms were full of fleas, so he said to his landlady, 'Are there any fleas in the room I've taken? Please be honest about it.' The landlady said there might be one.

Next day Paddy came down for breakfast with a huge smile on his face.

'I've good news for you,' he said. 'Your flea's dead.'

'That's great,' said the landlady, 'but how do you know it's dead?'

'I'm sure it's dead,' Paddy said, 'because all the fleas in the street attended his wake last night.'

THE POPE'S LUGGAGE

Paddy Irishman, Paddy Englishman and Paddy Scotsman were having the *craic* in the middle of a quiet country road when a coach and four came round a blind corner, mowed them down and killed them. The three of them flew straight up to heaven and asked St Peter to let them pass through the pearly gates. St Peter refused and told them to go straight down to hell and stop messing about at heaven's gates. Fortunately St Patrick appeared. He looked at Paddy Irishman and said, 'You're and Irishman, aren't you?' Paddy said he was and St Patrick said, 'One of my jobs in heaven is to judge Irishmen. I can see you've been a bit of a rascal during your life, but there's no real harm in you. You may enter heaven.'

Paddy Irishman asked if his friends could come with him. St Patrick said he was sorry, but he was not allowed to judge people from any nation other than Ireland. Paddy Irishman looked sadly at his companions and said he didn't want to go to heaven without them.

At that point, the Pope who had just died, arrived at heaven's gates and St Peter welcomed him with open arms.

Paddy Irishman turned to Paddy Englishman and said, 'I've an idea. Climb up on my back.'

Paddy Englishman did as he was asked.

Paddy Irishman turned to Paddy Scotsman and said, 'Now Paddy Scotsman, you climb on top of me as well.'

Paddy Scotsman also did as he was asked.

Paddy Irishman said, 'Right lads, keep your heads down.'

He walked straight up to the heavenly gates and gave them a good shake.

St Peter appeared and asked who they were.

Paddy Irishman shouted, 'The Pope's luggage.'

They were admitted.

15

WEE MEG BARNILEG
AND THE FAIRIES

*I was amazed the first time I visited Rochester, New York, to hear Sharon
Saluzzo tell this story, which she said came from County Fermanagh.
I had never heard it and, at the time, neither had any other storyteller in
Ireland, as far as I was aware. This is an example of a tale that crossed the
Atlantic, disappeared in Ireland and finally returned home. Sharon told
me that Ruth Sawyer, the author of* The Way of the Storyteller, *first
published by Penguin Books in 1976, had a nursemaid, called Johanna,
who had emigrated from Ireland and brought her stories with her.*

A long time ago a rich farmer and his wife lived beside Lough Erne.
They were a kindly, good-hearted pair who had one daughter, a wee
terror called Meg. She was spoilt rotten. Whatever she wanted she got.
Her parents doted on her. As far as they were concerned she could
do no wrong. Wherever they went they took Meg. She accompanied
them to fairs, weddings, wakes and festivals and she was guaranteed
to behave badly everywhere. The neighbours hated to see them
coming because she was a destructive child who would smash your
best china and she had a tongue fit for clipping hedges. When she
went visiting she'd stand in the middle of the floor and look around,
then turn to her mother and make comments such as, 'Do you see
they've still got them old torn lace curtains at the window? Thon
chair still has a broken leg and look at that! The dirt from the floor's
been brushed into the corner under yon brush. Thon's a disgrace.'

She was even worse at a wake, passing remarks such as, 'Listen til auld Aggie coughing her head off. Another clean shirt'll do her. I'll bet hers is the next wake we'll be enjoying. She's got consumption, so she has.'

And when she wasn't encouraging people into the grave she'd say things like, 'Didn't Barney Gallagher say before he died that Barney Maguire was the meanest man in the whole of Ireland? I remember father telling mother he'd rather strike a bargain with the auld devil himself than with him. Do ye remember saying, yon Father?'

When Meg wasn't pestering the neighbours she was pestering animals. She took delight in pulling the cat's tail and whiskers, beating dogs with sticks, pulling feathers out of hens and chickens and the wings off flies. She was a terror and she had her poor mother worn to the bone.

Her mother was a fussy woman, who took pride in her tidy house and well-dressed family. She spent her days cleaning up after Meg, who trailed mud into the house and went through clothes like a dose of salts. She had a special talent for becoming covered in dirt and tearing dresses. Every night her poor mother sat mending and sewing by candlelight.

Meg often refused to eat what was set in front of her.

'I can't stomach that rubbish!' she'd shout before throwing perfectly good food on the floor.

Her mother's soft voice was often heard wheedling, 'Meg, darling, tell me what you'd like to eat. You've got to keep your strength up. Please put that bowl down before you break it and stop annoying the dog. Now, come on, be a good girl and your da'll take you to the shop and buy you some sweeties.'

In other words, Meg's mother, without meaning to, encouraged her to behave badly.

The neighbours said, 'It's a disgrace what thon wean puts her mother through and her such a nice, gentle woman.'

One day Meg's mother decided to take Meg next door to the neighbouring farm to borrow a bowl of sugar. When the farmer's wife saw her coming she let out a cry that could be heard over the whole of Ireland.

'Lorny bless us! Here comes Meg. Quick, hide the new butter crock in the loft, put the best platter under the bed. Tie the pig in the byre, hide the hens' eggs in the churn and pray to the Holy Virgin we survive with nothing broken.'

Meg came into the house and looked around.

'Mother,' she said, 'do you see auld granny sitting in the corner there? She looks greyer than ever. I'll bet she's not long for this world. She'll soon be pushing up the daisies. Just look at thon boil she has on her eyelid! Have you ever seen anything so ugly? And do you see they've still got that old faded rug on her knee. They mustn't be doing too well or they'd get her a nice new one.'

Meg ran round the kitchen like a wild thing. A hen walked in through the open door. She kicked it and followed as it squawked and rushed back outside.

Old Jack, the gentlest dog in the whole of Fermanagh lay asleep in the street. Meg kicked him awake. Jack groaned, stood up and wagged his tail. Meg pulled his whiskers. Then she began to tease him by holding a bar of chocolate out and jerking it away as he went to eat it. Eventually Jack accidentally bit her and she went off like a siren before running back into the house screaming.

'Old Jack bit me! Old Jack bit me! He should be shot, so he should. He's a dangerous dog.'

She climbed on to her mother's knee and sobbed.

'There! There!' comforted her mother. 'Let me kiss you better. My poor wee darling! Did that nasty dog hurt you? You're right. He should be shot for biting my wee sweetheart.'

The farmer was attracted by the commotion and came into the kitchen.

'That child should be shot, not Jack,' he said firmly. 'Jack's the gentlest dog in the whole of Fermanagh, if not in the whole of Ireland. That child's a cruel wee hussy. If Jack bit her she deserved it.'

Meg peeped through her fingers. The farmer looked angry. He scowled at her. Would he really shoot her, she wondered. She felt uneasy and sat quietly on her mother's knee, then, when nobody was looking, she slithered down and sneaked out through the open door.

'That nasty old farmer'll never catch me!' she chortled as she struggled through a hole in the hedge and into the field. She ran and ran, aiming to get as far away from the house as possible. Eventually, after running through several fields, she saw men making hay. She watched for a few minutes before going to hide behind a haystack. She found their food in a pail covered with a dish in the shade there. She felt hungry and devoured everything she fancied. She threw the rest of the food on the ground before stopping and thinking, 'Maybe the men'll be angry when they see I've eaten their lunch. Perhaps they'll help the farmer catch and shoot me. Maybe I'd better hide.'

She went into another field, found another haystack and sat down behind it. The sun was very warm and Meg had had a lot of exercise. The drowsy sound of bees humming as they collected honey made her feel sleepy. She closed her eyes and fell into a deep slumber.

The men finished their work and went home to milk their cows, the sun set, bats flitted against the moon. Meg woke up with a start. She heard tinkling voices and felt confused. Who was there? Where was she? What had happened to her? She peeped in the direction of the voices and saw a troop of fairies dressed in green jackets and red hats, dragging small rakes.

A small voice complained, 'That terrible child's a blithering nuisance, scattering hay like this. We'll never get the place ready in time to have a decent dance before dawn.'

'Somebody should teach her some manners,' another said.

'Yes, and to be more thoughtful. I hate the way she wastes food and have you seen how she destroys clothes? She has her poor mother worn to the bone, what with cleaning and washing and ironing and mending. It's a crying shame.'

'Fairies dance and fairies sing.'

'I hope we catch her some night and have a chance to knock some sense in til her. Ye'll see! *Tiochaidh ár lá*! (Our time will come!) We'll teach her a lesson!'

Any other child would have been frightened to hear such a conversation, but not Meg. She was confident and used to having her own way and getting into the middle of everything.

'What can those silly wee fairy men do?' she thought. 'They're old and feeble. I'm bigger and stronger than they are. I'll teach them a lesson. I'll knock them down like ninepins before I go home.' With that she jumped out from behind the haystack.

'Come on!' she shouted. 'Who's going to teach me a lesson? You and what army?'

She ran around, knocking the melt out of the fairies and laughing her head off.

The night grew very silent. The wee men didn't say a word. They just looked solemnly and quietly at Meg. Then one shouted, 'Make the fairy ring! Make the fairy ring! Fairies dance and fairies sing!'

The wee men quickly formed a ring round Meg and began to dance. Their tiny feet wove complicated patterns on the green, green grass. Meg felt confused. The fairies moved so quickly they became a blur and she couldn't see one to catch. They raised their small voices in song. It was a lovely tune but somehow threatening.

Ring, ring in a fairy ring,
Fairies dance and fairies sing.
Round, round on soft green ground –
Never a sound, never a sound.
Sway, sway as the grasses sway,
Down by the lough at the dawn of day.
Circle about as we leap and spring
Fairy men in a fairy ring.
Light on your toe, light on your heel,
One by one in a merry, merry reel.
Fingers touching, fingers so –
Round and round and round we go!

When the song was finished the wee men clapped their hands, kicked their heels and spun round like a hundred green spinning tops. Then they shouted, 'Move hand or foot if ye can, wee Meg Barnileg.'

Meg found she couldn't move a muscle.

'Open your mouth and come out with some of those fine statements you're famous for,' jeered the fairies.

Meg opened her mouth to scream and found her tongue was stuck to the roof of her mouth. She couldn't utter a squeak!

'Now have a look at your substitute,' the fairies laughed. 'He'll make a fine changeling.'

With that the fairies went and brought out the ugliest wee man you could imagine. They laid him on the ground and laughed.

Meg was horrified. She'd heard of changelings but hadn't believed such things existed. She felt sick as she watched the fairies weave a spell. In the wink of an eye the ugly wee man grew and grew until he was the spitting image of Meg – face, hair, dress, boots, the lot. He stretched out in the hollow where Meg had been lying and was fast asleep before you could say, 'Jack Robinson!'

'Now,' shouted the wee men, 'it's time for you, my beauty. We'll take you below.'

A hundred pairs of fairy hands grabbed her, carried her over to a fairy thorn and threw her up in the air. Suddenly she was falling, falling, falling, down, down and down through a dark, black hole until she landed on a pile of soft leaves. She looked around and found she was at the heart of a fairy souterrain. A gentle light shone from what looked like thousands of glow-worms hanging around the walls and ceiling.

The place was beautiful but the floor was covered in scraps of food.

'You dirty clarts,' shouted Meg. 'If you'd any sense you'd keep this place clean and tidy the way my mother does at home!'

The fairies laughed heartily.

'Meg,' said their leader, 'that's all the food you've wasted in your life. Here's a rake. Brush it up. Eat it when you're hungry.'

'No! No! NO!' yelled Meg, stamping her foot in rage. 'I'll never eat that rubbish. I'm hungry. I want a drink of milk and a piece of currant cake.'

'Tough titty,' said the fairy leader firmly. 'You can't have any-thing fresh while all that wasted food lies uneaten. The quicker you eat it the quicker you'll have something fresh. It's up to you. You may starve if you choose. Here's the rake. Tidy the floor. Come on! Get moving! We can't dance on it the way it is.'

So Meg found herself with a rake in her hands.

The floor was covered as far as the eye could see with cold spuds, bits of wheaten bread, lumps of stirabout, soda farls, potato bread, crumbs of cake, half-eaten apples and whatnot. She raked the largest pieces into a corner and swept the smallest into tidy piles. She worked and worked until she was exhausted. Every joint in her body ached and she grew hungrier and hungrier.

'My belly thinks my throat's cut,' she yelled. 'If you're going to force me til work like a slave for ye, ye could at least have the manners til bring me something til eat.'

The fairies laughed, 'You've wasted all that good food and we've told you that we'll not give you a morsel until you use what you've wasted.'

In the end Meg's hunger forced her to eat her own leftovers. At last, weeks later, she'd finished her task and was given a piece of fresh bread and a drink of milk. It tasted wonderful. She vowed she'd never waste food again.

'Now, we've another wee job for you,' said a fairy, as he led her into another cavernous underground space. It was cluttered with dirty, torn dresses, every stitch she'd ever worn since she could first creep around the floor.

Meg looked about her, kicked one of her dresses and snarled, 'What do you want me to do with this lot?'

'Wash, iron and mend your clothes. You had your poor mother worn to a frazzle running around after you.'

'WON'T!' yelled Meg. 'WON'T! WON'T WON'T!'

She stamped her feet and stuck her tongue out as far as if would go.

'Meg,' said the wee man quietly, 'it's up to you. We can wait a thou-sand years for you to make amends.' And with that he disappeared.

Meg walked around in a temper, kicking clothes, banging walls with her fists and saying bad words. She threw herself on the ground and had a temper tantrum. Nobody came near her and she began to feel foolish. She picked herself up and thought, 'Maybe I should start washing, ironing and mending. At least it'd be something to do.'

The minute that thought crossed her mind an old fairy woman appeared, took her over to a washtub and showed her how to wash clothes. Meg began to scrub her dirty dresses. Her hands became red and sore as she washed and scrubbed. Then she had to starch and iron them. The iron was heavy and hot and she burnt herself several times. She hated mending. It was a boring job and the task seemed endless. The fairies were not sympathetic.

'Think of the trouble you gave your poor mother,' they said. 'Now that you're here she has peace and quiet to rest and the neighbours are enjoying life for the first time in years!'

At last Meg had finished and the fairies took her into a large space filled with the ugliest plants she'd ever seen. They looked like nettles with the thorns of thistles. Every here and there was a pretty flower.

'What's all that about?' asked Meg.

'Those weeds are all the nasty words you have ever spoken. You must pull them out and put them over there on the compost heap.'

'WON'T! WON'T! WON'T!' yelled Meg.

Immediately three large ugly plants appeared at her feet.

'You were shouting,' said the fairy. 'You must learn to guard your tongue or you'll never finish this task.'

Meg looked around her. Had she really been that nasty?

'What are those pretty flowers?' she asked

The fairy smiled, 'Sometimes you made a mistake and said something pleasant like telling your mother you loved her. They're all the nice words you have ever spoken.'

Meg felt ashamed for the first time in her life. Had she really said so few nice things and been so nasty? She got down on her knees and began weeding. It was a terrible job. The stings caused her hands to become swollen, her knees felt like two red lumps of burning turf, her back ached, her joints became sore and she learnt to control her tongue. Every time she said something nasty another ugly weed appeared. She began playing games with the space. When a fairy appeared she said something pleasant and watched as pretty flowers grew. At last she was finished. She looked around her and for the first time since she'd gone to live with the fairies she felt happy. The room looked very pretty with all those beautiful flowers. She lifted her skirts and began to dance with joy.

Fairies love dancing, so when they saw Meg bending and swaying like a flower and pointing her toes so nicely they clapped their hands and cheered.

'Meg?' they asked. 'Would you like to come above ground tonight and dance with us by the light of the silver moon?'

'I'd love to,' said Meg.

That night Meg, for the first time in a year, smelt new-cut hay and the fragrant roses blooming round cottage doors. She felt a soft balmy breeze caressing her cheek and saw the green grass under her feet. It was wonderful. Then she remembered her mother had once said, 'Anyone taken by the fairies can escape by finding a four-leaf clover and wishing to go home.'

Meg lifted her skirts and began to dance. She took every possible opportunity to bend down low and look for a four-leaf clover, but to no avail. She became homesick and her heart despaired as the moon sank behind the mountains, then she saw it outlined against her shiny, black patent shoe. A lucky four-leaf clover!

'Look,' she shouted in delight, as she held it up. 'Look what I've found! I can have a wish! I wish I was at home!'

With that she woke up in her own wee bed. Her mother was sitting beside her.

'Mother,' said Meg. 'I hope they didn't shoot the dog. He'd never have bitten me if I hadn't tortured the life out of him.'

Her mother looked at her in astonishment.

'Meg,' she said, 'you don't sound like yourself. What happened to you? We found you fast asleep behind a haystack in Nobel's field. That was a year ago today.'

Meg explained how she had been captured by the fairies and how they had taught her to behave herself.

From that day until the day she died Meg was a changed person. She was thoughtful, kind and gentle. She helped her mother tidy up, kept a civil tongue in her head and ate everything put before her. When she grew up she got married and had seventeen children. Today, if you walk along the banks of Lough Erne and see a well-behaved child the neighbours will probably tell you, 'That child is the great-great-great grandchild of wee Meg Barnileg.'

16

THE COONEEN GHOST

Thanks are due to the staff at the Westville Hotel, Enniskillen, for being the first to tell me about the Cooneen ghost and to Robena Elliott in the Enniskillen Library for telling me the story in greater detail.

The entry in the 1911 census of Ireland for Cornarooslan, County Fermanagh, records that Mrs Bridget Murphy, her son James (21) and her four daughters, Anne (18), Mary (16) Bridget (12), Catherine (7) and Jane-Anne (3), lived in the townland, but the entry hides a dark secret. The family were soon to be plagued by a poltergeist, which became known as the Cooneen ghost.

The Murphys moved into an isolated farmhouse in 1913. It was a comfortable, thatched cottage that had belonged to people called Burnside. They sold it to the Corrigan family, who passed it on to the Sherrys. The Sherry family were the first family to experience poltergeist activity. They only stayed there for one night and were so terrified they moved out, kept quiet about their experiences and six months later sold the house to the unsuspecting Murphys.

The ghost first made itself known to the Murphys shortly after Mrs Murphy's husband Michael fell out of a cart and was killed. At the time the death was thought to be freak accident but, in retrospect, people wondered if Michael's death had been the work of the ghost.

James went out to a ceili in a neighbour's house shortly after his father's death while the rest of the family enjoyed a quiet night at home. Mrs Murphy and Anne were sitting chatting beside the turf fire and the youngest daughters were in bed.

Suddenly they heard the children screaming in terror and a loud tapping on the walls and heavy footsteps.

At first Mrs Murphy and her daughter were not worried. They thought someone was playing a joke on them. When James came back home the three of them searched the house from top to bottom but found nothing. That was the beginning of the nightmare.

After that, the poltergeist made regular appearances. It began with occasional knocking on the front door. When members of the family went to answer it they found nobody there. There was a room above the house, which was used to store hay and was accessible by an outside stone staircase. Heavy footsteps were often heard coming from it, but, yet again, when one of them went to investigate there was nobody there.

Mrs Murphy invited her neighbours round to see if they had the same kind of experiences. They did, as did Cahir Healy, the MP for the area, who said, 'I simply could not believe what I was seeing.'

Eventually the family went to two priests, their own parish priest, Fr Patrick McKenna and Fr Peter Smyth, CC Cooneen, to see if they could help. The two gentlemen didn't see or hear anything. At a later date two other priests, Fr Coyle, a young curate at Maguiresbridge, and Fr Eugene Coyle CC, also of Maguiresbridge, came and attempted to help.

Fr Coyle said, 'I stood in the children's bedroom and watched bedclothes on an empty bed rise and fall as if someone was lying there. I felt a cold, evil presence, then pots and pans suddenly flew off the dresser onto the floor. On another occasion Fr Smith and I were standing side by side downstairs when we heard a crash coming from the storey above. I can't really describe what happened next. It felt as if a terrific blast of cold air rushed between us. We both felt it. It was very strange because it didn't disturb our clothing. We saw the ghost grab cups and saucers off the dresser and smash them on the floor. It snatched the bedclothes off the sleeping children and flung them across the room. At times the bed lifted several inches off the ground before falling back down again while mysterious shapes appeared and disappeared on the walls.'

Other observers heard the Cooneen ghost snore or make noises which appeared to come from far below the ground. It could hiss, whistle and make a sound like a kicking horse. It could also tap out tunes – its two favourites were 'The Solder's Song' and 'Boyne Water' – and reply to questions by tapping out answers.

Neighbours came to sit with the family at night and they all experienced the ghost's activity. Mrs Murphy moved the children's bedroom to the end of the house, but the ghost followed them. A respectable neighbour heard a noise coming first from one side of the children's bed, then the other and then from under the bed. This was followed by a scraping noise along the bed. The bed-clothes rose gently as if 'a dog or a pig was hoking in it.' He asked the little girl if she felt anything.

'Yes, I can feel something pressing down here,' she said as she put her hands on her tummy.

Father Coyle was given permission to perform two exorcisms in the house. They didn't work. The ghost continued to make sheets rise up off the beds, throw cups and plates around the room and issue deafening groans which appeared to come from upstairs. It seemed to be jeering at them.

The Murphys were terrified. They had hoped Fr Coyle would be able to get rid of it. To make matters worse the neighbours began to ostracise them. Rumours were rife, including one saying the ghost was that of a pensioner who had been murdered in the house.

Another rumour held that James Murphy had found a book in a forest near Cooneen called *The Legions of Doom* about the practice of satanic rites, how to contact demons and so on and that he had developed an unhealthy interest in the spirit world. He was supposed to have raised a demon. So it was said the Murphys had brought the entity on themselves. It served them right, so it did!

The malicious stories were the straw that broke the Murphy's back. They decided to leave Fermanagh and emigrate to America. They were relieved when they left their old home because they thought they had left the ghost behind. It was not to be. Halfway through their voyage they discovered it was still with them. Passengers complained about tapping and banging coming from the Murphys' cabin. The noises became so bad that the captain paid them a visit and demanded the family stop making such a racket. He didn't believe in ghosts or poltergeists, refused to credit what they told him and threatened to put them off ship if they didn't stop creating such an obnoxious noise.

The ghost continued to haunt the Murphys when they reached New York and they were forced to move house five times. It didn't leave them until 1915.

Was the Cooneen ghost the first ghost to cross the Atlantic in an emigrant ship? Was it the first Irish-American ghost?

17

LOUGH MELVIN AND THE RIVER SILLEES ARE CURSED

I obtained the story about St Febor and the noblemen from Linda
Ballard, who worked in the Ulster Folk and Transport Museum.
The story about the monk was found in Enniskillen Library.

Saint Febor was a kindly, gentle woman who, when roused, displayed a bit of a temper and a talent for cursing things.

She was busy with her work when the noblemen of County Fermanagh invited her to a feast. What that work was is not recorded. Perhaps she was planning what she was going to write as she was a fine scholar. Or perhaps she was simply wondering how to help someone who was poverty-stricken or sick. Anyway she was distracted as she travelled to the venue the noblemen had chosen, beside Lough Melvin.

The noblemen thought St Febor was a bit too hoity-toity for their liking. She didn't pay them much attention and seemed more interested in poor, unfortunate wretches they considered beneath their notice.

As for St Febor, she couldn't care less about the noblemen. They were stubborn pagans, beyond the call of reason, determined not to embrace Christianity. The only reason she had accepted her invitation was to avoid causing offence.

The noblemen knew that at that time Christians were not allowed to eat any meat on Fridays, although they were permitted to eat fish. They thought it would be a great joke to see a Christian saint eating forbidden meat on a Friday and decided to play a trick on her. She, as usual, wasn't paying any attention to them. It'd serve her right if they got her to carry out a forbidden act. They set her down at a table and brought her a large plate of chicken.

Saint Febor's eyes were on higher things than food. She sat down in an absent-minded fashion and was about to tuck into the chicken when she realised the noblemen were winking, nudging each other and laughing. She looked around to see what they found so amusing and saw the chicken on her plate. Obviously they were laughing their legs off at the sight of a saint who was about to eat meat on a Friday. She stood up in a terrible temper, cursed the

'I curse you.'

chicken on her plate and turned it into fish – not dead, cooked ones, but live ones. They leapt into Lough Melvin and became known as the 'gillaroo'. These fish are found only in Lough Melvin and strangely enough they have something resembling a chicken's gizzard inside and taste like chicken.

On another day St Febor and her pet fawn were walking along the bank of the River Sillees in County Fermanagh. She was very fond of it. It followed her around like a dog and went everywhere with her. She designed a satchel for it to carry on its back so it could carry her books.

One day as she and the fawn were walking along beside the River Sillees, a hunter and his dogs came along. They frightened the fawn, causing it to jump into the river. Saint Febor's books were ruined and she was furious. She was not annoyed with the hunter, his dogs or the fawn, but with the River Sillees. She stood on its bank and shouted, 'The River Sillees will from this day forth be good for drowning and bad for fishing.'

That curse has endured to the present day. Every year people drown in the river.

Saint Febor isn't the only person held responsible for the gillaroo in the Lough Melvin. Folklore also attributes them to an ancient monk who had been fasting. When he ended his fast, he was famished, so he went fishing in the river. He fished and fished and fished, but caught nothing. Eventually he pulled a duck egg and a small eel out of the water. He was upset because that was not sufficient to satisfy his hunger. He made a cross in the sand and placed the egg and the eel in it to prevent them from moving away. (Folklore holds that this had a significant effect on the eel's psyche because, from that day to this, eels in Lough Melvin will not attempt to escape from a cross drawn in the sand!)

The old monk was in despair as he looked at the egg and the eel, so he prayed to be rewarded for his fast. When he opened his eyes he found the duck egg and the eel had turned into two golden-bellied fish. He couldn't bear to eat them so he set them free to multiply in the lough.

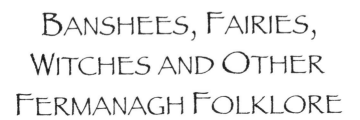

18

BANSHEES, FAIRIES, WITCHES AND OTHER FERMANAGH FOLKLORE

Thanks are due to the late Dr Johnston, who originally came from Fermanagh, and to Vicki Herbert for the story about gold hidden in the grounds of Crom Castle. I am also indebted to the late Jim McVeigh for collecting folk tales around the Ederney District from 1939 and 1940. He was born in Moneyvriece, Ederney, on 11 September 1918 and died at his home in Enniskillen, on 20 February 1990. His nephew published his work and I have found them very useful.

BANSHEES

The banshee is a figure of dread who warns old Irish families about impending death. She can appear as a beautiful woman or as a terribly ugly old hag. She is seen sitting on walls, trees or bushes, crying, sighing and wringing her hands. Perhaps she's remembering her own death, which would have been far from pleasant. She could have been murdered, involved in a fatal accident or she might have died suddenly of a fever.

Dr Johnston was born in Fermanagh. Some time after he qualified as a doctor he joined a medical practice in Portaferry, which is where I met him in the 1990s. He was an old, respected gentleman and he told me about his experiences with banshees. According to him, the banshee's prophecy is not always correct. He told me the following story to prove his point.

When he first came to Portaferry he became very fond of Miss Johnston, one of his elderly patients. She was not a relative, although they had the same surname. Miss Johnston was a lovely old lady who lived alone. She had been very ill and he made a habit of calling in to see her to make sure she was all right. She was normally a cheerful woman who always offered to 'give him a wee cup of tea in his hand'. One day he found her sitting at the fireside, crying her eyes out. He asked her what was wrong and she said, 'Last night the banshee sat in the trees opposite my bedroom window and cried and cried. I just know my brother, who lives in America, is dead.'

Dr Johnston did his best to comfort her but to no avail. He was still with her when a telegram boy arrived. In those days (1939, just before declaration of the Second World War), there were few telephones so urgent messages were sent via Morse code to the post office. They were written down and given to telegram boys, who were employed to ride their bicycles as fast as possible from the post office to the recipient of the message. The boys were smartly dressed in navy-blue uniforms with red trimmings and buttons and a smart navy-blue, red-trimmed pill-box hat. The news they brought was generally bad, so people dreaded seeing one coming.

Dr Johnston took the telegram and held it out to Miss Johnston. She was trembling so much that she could not open it, so she asked him to open it and read it to her. It said Miss Johnston's brother had suffered a severe heart attack and was not expected to live. However, this story has a happy ending. The brother survived and Miss Johnston was able to visit him after the war.

Dr Johnston said, 'Strange things happen. At the time I dismissed such stories about banshees, fairies, ghosts and so on as coincidences or just stuff and nonsense. I had a scientific training and thought I knew better. Now I'm not so sure. I feel there's another dimension of which we are not normally aware. I can still recall a strange experience I had when I was a young doctor working on the border between Fermanagh and Tyrone. I was called out, in the middle of the night, by the McGirr family because the father had taken ill suddenly. He had had a stroke and he died shortly after I arrived.

'I was in the process of writing a death certificate at eight o'clock in the morning when the phone went. Phones were a rare commodity at the time but the McGirrs were a wealthy family. They owned a pub and they had one. Their daughter was on the line. She had a good job in New York and she was in tears. She said, "I know something terrible's happened to Dad because the wee lady (she meant the banshee) woke me up a few minutes ago. She's sitting on the wall of my apartment and crying and crying and crying."

'Her mother had to tell her that her father had been dead for about thirty minutes.

'Now, when you think about it, that's strange. The time in New York is five hours behind Northern Ireland. Something had wakened that girl up in the middle of the night. Something had told her all was not well with her father and that something was quite correct. It's not as if her father was poorly. He appeared to be in good health and his sudden death came as a terrible shock to the family.

'At the time I thought the whole thing was a coincidence but my life has been too full of coincidences for me to think there's any such thing.'

The crying of a banshee, which is also known as keening, is similar to a sound which can be made by a fox vixen.

Years ago, when I was storytelling in a nursing home in Lisnaskea, an old man became angry with an elderly woman who was telling me about hearing three knocks on her wall, which she claimed informed her a neighbour 'had departed'.

The old man shouted, 'That's a lot of baloney! I once thought I heard a "banshee" crying outside my window, but I've got a bit of sense. I looked out and there was a vixen carrying on, on top of my wall. I got my gun out and shot it! Huh! Some banshee!

'And I'll tell you something else. I don't believe in ghosts either!

'One night I'd been at a wedding and I came home late. Pitch black it was. When I reached the door of my house I heard a low, loud groan. I thought the devil had come to claim me soul, so I did. The hairs on the back of my neck rose up and I started til shiver with fear. I saw something move at the gate beside my house. I let a big squeal outta me, but then I caught myself on. Says I til myself, says I, "There's more spirits in me than are without of me," and I lifted a big stick til bate the melt out of any intruder and marched towards the gate. And do you know? It was my poor auld cow. I'd been out all day and I had neglected til milk her. I'd been having so much *craic* I'd forgotten all about her, the poor auld baste. Once I'd milked her she was fine and dandy.

'I'm tellin' ye, there ain't no such thing as banshees, fairies or ghosts or any of that auld-fashioned nonsense.

'All ye need til do is have the guts til go and look for a logical explanation.'

FAIRY LORE

In the olden days people spoke unselfconsciously about fairies. Their existence was taken for granted. Fairies were said to live in the 'gentle places', such as under fairy thorns, in underground caves called souterrains and in prehistoric monuments such as raths, cairns and dolmens. They were taken very seriously and people thought they should leave fairies in peace to prevent bad luck. In Ireland today the majority of people say they do not believe in fairies, but they won't take any chances. I, for one – and I am not alone – would never interfere with a fairy thorn or one of the old places. And come to think of it, I wouldn't risk being near either of them after dark.

Fairies love beauty and luxury. They hate meanness, such as the hand that gathers the last grain, plucks the trees bare of fruit and drains the last drop from the milk pan, leaving nothing for the spirits who wander around during the night. They like food and wine to be left out for them. They might want a bath, so you should leave out enough pure water for them to bathe in. If you treat fairies well they will bring you good luck.

In Ireland it used to be considered unlucky to demolish an old house because the 'old people' – that is the spirits of those who had once lived in the house – like to come and sit by the fire at night after everyone has gone to bed. It would be unkind to deprive them of their familiar surroundings. That's the reason there are so many old houses in Ireland that haven't been knocked down and have been left to decay. People shouldn't stay up too late because the fairies also like to come in and sit round the fire after everyone is asleep.

Fairies have a habit of stealing human children, so if ever a mother has to leave her baby asleep the fire irons should be placed across the cradle to protect it. This is particularly important for babies who have not been baptised because fairies find it very easy to seize them. Another preventative is to tie a little salt into the baby's clothes before it is laid down to sleep in its cradle.

When fairies are successful in carrying off a baby they may leave a poor weak child, known as a 'changeling', in its place. The fairies will bring the child back to its parents if it grows up to be ugly because they worship beauty and don't like ugly people.

J. Carroll, who lived in Edenticromman, was coming home one night when he saw a wee man, wearing a red jacket, standing outside the window of a house. He knew there was a baby inside that had not been baptised. To his horror he spotted another wee man inside the house in the process of passing the baby out the window. Carroll ran to the scene, pushed the wee man aside, grabbed the baby and ran home with it. Next day he heard a baby had died in the house where he had seen the fairies. He visited the child's parents and found them crying their eyes out. He told them the dead baby was a changeling and suggested they put it on a shovel and hold it over the fire. They followed the suggestion and the changeling disappeared up the chimney. The parents were overjoyed to find that their child was safe.

Fairy chiefs long for pretty, human brides so handsome girls must be well guarded to prevent them from being stolen and married off to a fairy. The children of such marriages may be recognised by their beautiful hair and eyes. They have a gift for music and song that is irresistible but they are wild, reckless and extravagant.

Barney Monaghan, who lived near Ederney, had a hump on his back. One day he decided to go to a shoemaker, who lived in Tummery. He had a pair of boots that needed to be mended. It was getting dark when he started on his return journey. He had travelled some miles when he heard the sweetest music in all the world. He was curious and went in the direction of the sound. Eventually he found the Queen of the Fairies sitting under a fairy thorn. She was beautiful. She sent two small men forward to lead Barney over to her.

'Can you sing?' she asked.

'I can that,' Barney replied.

'Can you dance?'

'I can indeed.'

'Well then,' said the Queen, 'let the hump be taken from your back.'

Local tradition recounts that from that day forward Barney Monaghan was a straight man.

There was a man by the name of Hamilton, who also had a hump. He heard how Barney had been cured and came to find out what had happened. Barney told him all about his visit to the fairies. Hamilton was delighted to find such an easy way to get rid of his hump and set off to hear the fairy music. He waited in the right spot and sure enough he heard the sweet music and was led to the queen.

'Can you sing?' asked the queen.

'No!' replied Hamilton.

'Can you dance?'

'No.'

'Oh,' said the queen, 'that's terrible. You can't dance and you can't sing so you'll have to have Barney Monaghan's hump on your back.' From that day until the day he died, poor Hamilton had two humps on his back.

Jim McVeigh recorded that story in 1937. He said it happened about a 120 years ago. I write this in 2014, so now it must be about 200 years old.

Thomas Carleton came from Oghill and lived to be a very old man. One evening, when he was a child, his mother went to Ederney. While she was away he heard beautiful music. He was curious, so he followed the sound, which led him to the gate of a field in which there was a 'gentle tree'. There were lots of the 'wee people' under the tree. Some were dancing and singing, others were playing violins and some were riding ponies. Tom was delighted and watched them for a long time. When he thought he heard his mother returning home he turned round, but there was nobody there. When he looked back through the gates the fairies had disappeared.

There was a man by the name of Turner, from Affagriffin, Kesh, who worked for a man called Johnston. Turner was ordered to clear several 'gentle' bushes from a small mound. A few days later he became ill and was tortured by sharp pains. He was bedridden until two wee men came to visit him. One was a little taller than the other and they stood, in silence, looking at Turner for some time until the smaller one said, 'He's suffered enough.'

'Look at what he done!' replied the taller one. 'Leave him be! He should be punished.'

There was an argument, the smaller man won and Turner became well enough to be up and about the very next day.

The Mystery Cow that Wandered between Sligo and Pettigo

About 200 years ago a beautiful white cow began to wander along the road between Sligo and Pettigo. She always chose to graze in the best field in the district. For example, in Castle Caldwell she stayed in a field known as Portahone in Garvery so people called her 'Gaskevenur'. She was a complete mystery because nobody knew where she came from and nobody claimed ownership of her. All anybody knew was that she allowed strangers to milk her and appeared whenever milk was scarce. It was odd because she had plenty of milk for everyone, no matter how many came to her. Many said she was a good fairy in disguise. Once milk became plentiful she disappeared as quickly as she had come.

WITCHCRAFT

There was a young boy who lived in poverty with his old grand-mother on an island in Lough Erne. The winter became icy and the poor wee lad had no boots. His feet were freezing and turned blue with cold. During a snowstorm a crowd of huntsmen appeared. The old lady turned to her grandson and said, 'Go and tell the huntsman you'll show them where a hare is hidden if they'll give you the price of a pair of boots.'

The lad did as he was told. He looked miserable. The huntsmen felt sorry for him and gave him money for boots. The boy took the huntsmen into a garden, as his granny had told to do. He pointed at a clump of rushes and said, 'There's a hare in there.'

The hare leapt out and the hounds gave chase. She ran round and round the garden. The dogs couldn't catch her and one of the huntsmen became suspicious. 'Was that a real hare?' he wondered. Then he realised it was a witch who had changed shape. The only bullet that can wound a witch is one made of silver so he put a silver sixpence in his gun and fired it at the hare as she ran through a gap in the hedge. He hit her back leg. She began to limp. The hounds ran towards her and the boy shouted,

'Run, Granny! Run or you'll dear buy the shoes!'

Later that day one of the huntsman peeped through the window of the grandmother's cottage and saw the old lady dressing a wound on her leg.

CHURNING AND WITCHES WHO STEAL BUTTER

Part of my childhood was spent living on the Castlereagh Road in Belfast. Somewhere near the old Castle Cinema there was a strange shop. The owner came from County Fermanagh. He sold what was known as 'country butter', which he obtained from his Fermanagh relatives and sold on what was known as the 'black market'. Food was rationed both during and after the Second World War so obtaining extra butter was illegal. Buying that delicious butter was worth the risk. When you tasted it, it felt like you had died and gone to heaven. It was different from the ration butter bought in proper grocery shops. It had a flavour all its own.

You could say the shop was 'different' to other shops. All the goods were piled in a huge heap in the middle of the floor. The place looked dingy and not too clean. You could buy all sorts of hardware there, including washers for leaking taps, mousetraps, screws, nails and, strangely enough, sewing needles. Although the place looked like it was in a shambles, it must have been organised because the proprietor could produce anything required in a matter of seconds! The butter was hidden from the authorities by wrapping it in clean sheets of greaseproof paper and keeping it in the middle of the pile.

Butter was sold by farmers' wives and was an important part of the rural economy. Anything that interfered with the production of good butter was considered a tragedy and was often blamed on the 'butter witch'. She was said to be able to turn butter sour and inedible and to make milk refuse to turn into butter, no matter how long it was churned. The following customs were thought to prevent terrible things happening to your butter.

Anybody entering a house while churning is taking place should say, 'Good luck to the cows and milk', then help with the process by taking a turn to wield the churn dash.

'The butter witch stole my milk!'

Cutting a piece of a person's coat and burning it under the cow's nose made that person unable to steal your butter.

Anyone judging your cow and touching her udder should say, 'She's a great cow. Good luck!' Failure to say, 'Good Luck!' was thought to lead to a failure in milk production.

Some people didn't like to see certain people gazing at their cows or walking across their land in case this resulted in a failure in milk production.

There once was a family who lived in Derrylin and had ten cows. Their cows produced so much milk that they churned every single day. One day they found it impossible to turn their milk into butter so they sent for a man known as 'Peter the Witch'.

Peter said, 'I'll bring the culprit to the door, but it'll be a "tight fight". One of us will have to leave this earth.'

The next day the man he blamed for stealing butter broke his neck while on the road to Lisnaskea.

A woman who lived in Meenbog sent for Fr Kelly because she found it impossible to turn her milk into butter.

Fr Kelly listened to her sad story and said, 'If you want to make the person who's stealing your butter burst into flames and come to your door, I'll tell you what to do.'

'How do you do that?' asked the woman.

'Get a donkey's shoe, heat it until it becomes red hot and put it under the churn. It'll make the person who's stealing your butter burst into flames and burn.'

Fr Kelly stayed silent for several minutes. He had a pensive look on his face. Then he said, 'On second thoughts I don't think you should do that. What you should do is keep your byre door locked and don't lend anything to anyone.'

There was a woman by the name of Weir, who lived close to Ederney. She had only one cow but she sold many pounds of butter at the market. She was busy churning one day when she dropped dead. The neighbours came in and looked into the churn. There was a large quantity of butter inside, much more than even three times the amount of milk one cow would yield usually. They were both shocked and amazed. She looked like a normal decent wee woman but she must have been a witch who was able to steal butter.

Dan Kearns went to work in England and returned to Fermanagh on a fine May morning. He was a great walker and used to walk from Dundalk to where he lived in Kinawley. In those days there wasn't any public transport, apart from the stagecoach. Bicycles hadn't been invented. If you wanted to go anywhere you went on shanks' pony – in other words, you walked. People thought nothing of walking thirty miles as they were much fitter than we are today.

Dan was walking along the road, minding his own business, when he spotted a woman in a field pulling a whin bush and saying, 'Cow's milk, mare's milk and anything e'r had milk come to me.'

Dan looked hard at her and shouted, 'Aye and half to me.'

The woman must have been frightened because she rushed off as if the hens of hell were after her, as indeed they might have been. Dan went over to the small bush she had been pulling, lifted it up and took it home. His cottage had a half loft in the kitchen. He threw the bush up there and forgot about it.

Some time later the butter in his churn became so thick he couldn't pull the churn dash up. He knew something was wrong and felt he had been subjected to an evil spell. He told his parish priest, who thought for several minutes before asking, 'Have you any bushes or anything like that in the house?'

At first Dan could think of nothing, then he remembered the whin bush in the loft and told the priest about it.

The priest said, 'Away home, get hold of that bush and burn it.'

Dan did as he was told. He had never seen the likes of the sparks that flew out of it nor heard a noise like that of the crackles as it burnt.

From that day until the day he died Dan had no more trouble with his butter.

19

THE FERMANAGH MYSTERY FOUND IN KILLADEAS CHURCHYARD

This is a strange tale. I feel I have always known it. I can't remember where I first heard it or who told it. I suspect it was my Granny Henry as I sat cuddled up against her on her big sofa beside a blazing fire. Imagine my amazement when I told the story in a school in New Brunswick, New York, to find it had a strange effect on one of the teachers. She told me it made the hairs on the back of her neck stand on end. She said that she came from the Gulf of Mexico and that in her culture there is a similar story about wizards who came across the sea in a ship made of white rock. The wizards had escaped from an evil land that is now submerged under the area of the sea known as the Bermuda Triangle. I like the underlying message of the story that we should take care of our environment.

The Atlantic Ocean once surrounded an enchanted island ruled by a magical people called the Tuatha Dé Danann. They were a proud and arrogant people. They called themselves the People of the Goddess Danu. They were wizards and they drew their power from the heart of the earth, which formed the core of their isle, so they could control the elements. They, like many people today, believed the earth had unlimited resources and so they squandered magic foolishly.

The Atlantic Ocean loved the goddess Danu and grew annoyed with the Tuatha Dé Danann. He strongly objected to her name being associated with a senseless waste of power. 'Why don't those fools realise that every stupid piece of wasted magic threatens to destroy their land and their very existence?' he snarled as he crashed waves upon the shore.

He was young and passionate and nurtured a profound love of the goddess. He became so angry that his rage boiled over and a desire for revenge entered his breast. He developed an insatiable thirst for knowledge as he sought to learn enough magic to defeat the wizards. He listened carefully to the spells they cast as they controlled the elements.

The Tuatha Dé Danann continued misusing power until the mountains that formed a ring around the enchanted isle started to erupt, throwing dust and smoke into the air. Rivers were poisoned, soil became lifeless and the seabed burned with fire as the earth was torn apart.

As the situation on the isle deteriorated wiser members of the Tuatha Dé Danann began to feel guilty. They realised they had abused power and that time was beginning to run out for them. They attempted to calm the Atlantic's anger by offering human sacrifices to the sea, the land and the fire mountains. The Atlantic Ocean was so angry he would not be appeased. He received their offerings and made them his own by absorbing their knowledge. He continued to rage against the isle, flooding fields and pounding cliffs. The mountains continued to erupt, belching out smoke, dust, fire and poisonous gases. The earth shook and the tempest roared.

Thirty-three of the most powerful wizards realised the serious-ness of the situation and decided to attempt to escape. They left the isle in a metal ship. The Atlantic Ocean roared with rage, drowned the wizards and swallowed the ship. He accepted their bodies as part payment for the way they had treated the love of his life, the goddess Danu, and for all the filth and poisons they had poured into him.

The Atlantic Ocean became even more powerful after he'd absorbed the knowledge from the minds of the drowned wizards and knew he could, at last, destroy the whole isle and everything that lived on it. The goddess Danu felt this was foolish and pleaded with him.

'If you drown everyone on the isle, nobody will remember what happened there. Please, please let at least some of the wizards escape. I think they've learnt a lesson. With any luck they'll teach people in other lands how important it is to take good care of the earth.'

Some of the Tuatha Dé Danann built boats of silver and fled for their lives. The Atlantic Ocean did as the Goddess Danu had suggested and destroyed the evil enchanted isle but allowed the wizards to escape. Some went to the lands of the west the inhabitants accepted them as gods. Others headed east and found a tiny island which was inhabited by humanoids, beasts and primitive man. Eventually that island came to be known as Erin.

The people of the goddess Danu ruled Erin for generations. They were powerful and could have gone on to conquer the known world but due to their experiences with the Atlantic Ocean, they were too frightened to leave their island and venture across the sea. Traces of their existence have been preserved in the strange figures, resembling those of the Aztecs, found in County Fermanagh and in the magic that laps the coast of Erin.

20

HUDDON, DUDDON
AND DÓNAL O'LEARY

*Linda Ballard gave me this crazy story, which is a cross between a
tall tale and a fireside story. I loved the way Linda told it. She made
the unlikely characters and the talking magpie seem real. She said
she got it from Henry Glassie, who recorded it from Fermanagh
resident Hugh Nolan in 1972. It, like 'Wee Meg Barnileg and the
Fairies', is full of implicit moral lessons that teach children how to
behave without preaching. More importantly, it's a fun story!*

Huddon, Duddon and Dónal O'Leary were farmers who lived
next door to each other a long time ago. Huddon and Duddon
were twins and Dónal O'Leary was their cousin. The twins lived
with their mother, whom they neglected, while Dónal O'Leary
also lived with his mother, but he took very good care of her.

Although they were blood relatives, Huddon, Duddon and
Dónal O'Leary had different outlooks on life. Dónal O'Leary was
a hard worker who got up at dawn and spent his days working on
his farm. Huddon and Duddon were lazy. They crawled out of
bed in the mid-morning. Their farm looked neglected and they
fed their old mother a few scraps around lunchtime. Their cow
was also neglected. She spent a lot of time looking forlornly over
the fence separating the two farms. She wished she lived on the
other side like Daisy, Dónal O'Leary's fat, well-fed cow. Daisy was
milked regularly and housed in a dry, comfortable cowshed, not

the draughty, uncomfortable hut, with its leaking roof, in which she dwelt.

Hutton and Dutton were jealous of Dónal's farm.

'Look!' they said to each other. 'Dónal's place is always neat and tidy while ours is a mess. His thatch is in perfect condition and look at the state of his fields! He's growing more vegetables than he can use.

'Why does his land always produce fine big potatoes while ours are the size of marbles? And look at the size of his cabbages! They're huge. The white butterfly never lays her eggs on them. It's not fair, so it's not.'

It never struck the twins that the difference between the two farms lay in their laziness and Dónal's hard work. Eventually they became so jealous they decided to take drastic action.

'Look at that big fat cow,' snarled Hutton. 'Dónal O'Leary loves that cow. He calls it Daisy and he's always fussing round her. Let's kill her. That'll annoy him. It's time he had some bad luck. He's far too smug for his own good.'

'Good idea,' agreed Dutton. 'We'll kill her tonight.'

After dark Hutton and Dutton sneaked into Dónal O'Leary's field and murdered poor Daisy.

The next day when he awoke Dónal O'Leary looked out the door and saw Daisy lying on the grass with her feet in the air.

'Daisy!' he yelled as he ran towards her. 'What's wrong?'

But Daisy couldn't answer. She was as dead as a dodo and the dead are never any good at answering questions!

Dónal O'Leary was devastated. He sat down and cried and cried, then he began to think and think and think.

'Dónal O'Leary,' he said to himself, 'catch yourself on. You loved old Daisy and now she's gone. There's no use in crying over spilt milk. Pull yourself together, man, and see what you can do to make the best of a bad situation … You could have Daisy butchered and smoked. You'd have the luxury of eating meat all winter. Mother'd enjoy that. And I'll tell you another thing. You could make a mint of money by selling her skin. You must remember it's not what happens to you in life – it's how you react to it and every cloud has a silver lining.'

So Dónal got up, swung Daisy over his shoulders and set off to town.

It was a sweltering hot day, Daisy was heavy and he began to feel parched.

'I could do with a drink,' he muttered. 'I'm boiling!'

He stopped at the pub, which was by the roadside on the way into town. He propped Daisy against the wall and walked towards the door. He was within a few steps of it when out came a magpie.

'Good morning,' said the magpie.

'Good morning,' said Dónal O'Leary, who was always polite, 'I didn't know that magpies could talk.'

'You don't know a lot and that's the truth,' said the bird.

'That's true,' replied Dónal O'Leary. 'I don't know a lot.'

'I like you,' said the magpie. 'You're an honest lad. But why are you carrying a dead cow?'

'I don't know what happened to poor Daisy. It was really bad luck. She was fine yesterday, God bless her wee cotton socks. I found her lying dead in the field this morning. I decided to make the best of a bad situation by taking her to market. I'm going to sell her skin and have her body butchered and smoked. Old Mother and I may as well have the luxury of eating meat all winter.'

'Can you do what you're told?' asked the magpie.

'Sure I can.'

'Well, go into the pub and do as I tell you. Begin by putting me into your pocket.'

Dónal O'Leary picked the magpie up, slipped it into his pocket, went into the pub, stood at the bar and smiled at the pretty barmaid, who came over and asked what he'd like to drink. The magpie jumped out of his pocket and said, 'He'll have a double whiskey.'

'I'll what!' gasped Dónal, who had never had a double whiskey in the whole of his life.

'You'll do as you're told and have a double whiskey,' snapped the bird.

The barmaid smiled at Dónal O'Leary.

'Mine's a double whiskey, like the bird says,' said Dónal O'Leary.

The barmaid was pretty. The pub's owner had told her if she didn't recognise a customer, or if he wasn't a regular, to distract his attention from what he was drinking by flirting with him and watering his whiskey. She did as she had been told, fetched Dónal O'Leary a diluted double whiskey and smiled at him.

Dónal O'Leary grinned and went to take a sip. The magpie flew into a rage.

'You're being cheated!' the bird squawked. 'That whiskey is bad. It's been watered. Give my owner a decent drink immediately. Cheat! Cheat! Cheat! CHEAT!'

The magpie kicked up such a din the owner came to see what was happening.

'What's up?' he asked.

The magpie leapt on Dónal O'Leary's shoulder and whispered into his ear,

'Tell him you've been served watered whiskey and you want a decent drop.'

Dónal O'Leary did as he was told and the magpie jumped onto the counter and began walking up and down talking to the customers.

The pub owner was intrigued.

'Where did that marvellous bird come from? Is it yours?'

Dónal started to say he had just met the magpie outside the pub. It jumped on his shoulder and whispered, 'Yes, I am! Tell the man that, and when he asks if you'll sell me say you will.'

'B-b-but –' stuttered Dónal O'Leary.

'Do as you're told,' commanded the magpie.

So Dónal O'Leary did as he was told and, as a result, was given thirty pieces of silver in exchange for the magpie.

As he went out the door Dónal O'Leary saw poor Daisy lying against the wall.

'I was going to sell the body of my cow,' he yelled to the pub owner. 'I don't need the money so you may have her as a luck penny. You can use her to make meat pies for your customers.'

Dónal O'Leary could not wait to get home to tell his old mother what had happened. She laughed and laughed and laughed with pleasure and they spent a happy evening counting and re-counting the thirty pieces of silver. They were so happy they began to sing. The noise attracted Hutton and Dutton, who came over to see what was going on.

Dónal O'Leary explained, 'I was so unhappy this morning when I awoke to find poor Daisy lying dead in the field. I decided there was no point crying over spilt milk and carried her body into town to have it butchered and smoked. I thought we'd eat her over the winter. It seemed a pity to let her body go to waste by burying it. When I reached town I discovered there's a war on. Dead cows are needed to feed the troops so I was given thirty pieces of silver for Daisy. Finding Daisy dead like that was a great piece of luck.'

Hutton and Dutton were annoyed.

'We don't believe you,' they snarled.

'See for yourself. I've got thirty pieces of silver. Where would I have got them if I wasn't telling the truth?'

Hutton and Dutton were filled with a mixture of rage and greed. They were raging because they had wanted to annoy Dónal O'Leary and their nasty action had brought him good luck and made him a wealthy man. On the other hand, he had found a ready market for a dead cow. There was a war on. Troops need to be fed during wartime. Food would be in short supply. That made perfect sense. They should kill their cow and sell her body. So Hutton and Dutton went home, slaughtered their cow and took it into town. Their cow was badly kept and scrawny so nobody bought it and they returned home in a terrible temper.

'It's not fair! Dónal O'Leary has all the luck,' moaned Dutton.

'He's a real pain in the neck,' groaned Hutton. 'It doesn't matter what happens to him. Everything always turns out for the best. It's not fair. Let's kill him.'

'Good idea!' replied Dutton. 'Let's creep into his house after dark and strangle him. That'll teach him a lesson.'

Of course Dónal O'Leary didn't know what his cousins were planning. All he knew was that the days were on the turn. There was a nip in the air, the leaves on the trees were beginning to drop and the nights were growing colder. His cottage had two rooms: a kitchen with the bright fire burning on the hearth and a cosy bed tucked into the wall beside it and a cold bedroom. Dónal let his mother sleep in the bedroom when the weather was hot. She was comfortable there while he was too warm sleeping beside the fire. After Daisy died the weather turned frosty and mother complained of the cold so Dónal O'Leary suggested they swap beds so she'd be nice and cosy in the warmth of the kitchen beside the fire.

Hutton and Dutton crept into Dónal O'Leary's cabin in the middle of the night, went over to the bed by the fire, grabbed hold of the body and strangled it.

Next day Dónal O'Leary woke up feeling worried. Something was wrong. The house was too quiet. He went into the kitchen and was surprised to find mother still in bed. He touched her gently. Her body was as cold as stone. She was dead. He was terribly upset. He loved his old mother so he sat down and had a good cry, then he began to think and think and think.

'Mother was very old,' he thought, 'and she was a good woman. She'll go straight to heaven. She died happy because thanks to that magpie she was rich. I'll be able to give her a decent funeral. I'll take her into town and give her a burial with all the trimmings. I'll miss her terribly but I must think positively and remember I was lucky to have such a great mother for such a long time.'

Dónal O'Leary picked his mother up and headed towards town. It was a warm day and as he passed the pub he felt thirsty so he propped mother against the wall and headed towards the door. The magpie came out to meet him.

'What happened?' it asked.

'I don't know,' Dónal O'Leary replied. 'Mother was happy when she went to bed last night but she didn't get up this morning because she was dead.'

'That's a good reason not to get up early in the morning,' said the magpie.

'Yes,' said Dónal O'Leary. 'She must have died during the night. Thanks to you I have enough money to give her a decent burial so I'm taking her into town to arrange a funeral.'

'Tell you what,' said the magpie. 'Take your mother and prop her up over there beside the well. Put her with her back to the pub's door. Go into the pub, order a drink for yourself and ask the bartender to take a drink of tea out to your mother. Tell him she is a respectable woman who never goes into a pub.'

'B-b-but don't you realise? She can't drink tea. She's dead. It's difficult to drink tea when you're dead,' Dónal O'Leary stuttered.

'Never mind that,' snapped the magpie. 'Do as you're told.'

So Dónal O'Leary did as he was told. He went into the pub, ordered a double whiskey for himself and a drink of tea to be carried outside to his mother.

The bartender served Dónal O'Leary and put a cup of tea on a tray for Dónal's mother.

'Mother'd like a piece of cake as well,' shouted the magpie, 'and remember Dónal O'Leary gave you the carcass of a cow yesterday so the drinks are on the house. And the old lady's deaf, so you'll have to speak up.'

The bartender was a mean man. He didn't like giving anything to anyone but felt obliged to obey the magpie. It could talk and might put an evil spell on him if he didn't do as it asked. He prepared a dainty tray with a delicious piece of lemon drizzle cake and carried it out to mother.

'Old lady,' he said, 'I've brought you a nice cup of tea.'

The old lady did not reply. It's difficult to reply when you're dead.

The bartender remembered the old lady was deaf so he repeated loudly, 'OLD LADY, I'VE BROUGHT YOU A NICE CUP OF TEA.'

There still was no response, so the bartender yelled at the top of his voice.

'OLD LADY, I'VE BROUGHT YOU A NICE CUP OF TEA!'

The old lady still did not pay any attention. She was dead and it's difficult to pay attention when you're dead. The bartender touched her arm. The old lady lost her balance and toppled upside down into the well. The bartender panicked and called for the owner. The owner was terribly upset. A death on the premises is not good for business.

'Help! Help! Help! The old lady's fallen into the well! Help me get her out!' he shouted.

It was difficult to get the old lady out of the well. She kept falling back down. Eventually they managed to haul her out and lay her on the grass. She looked as if she had been drowned. They tried artificial respiration and everything they could think of, but the old lady was definitely dead. The pub owner rushed to Dónal O'Leary.

'I'm so sorry. Your mother fell into the well. We managed to get her out, but – b-b-but … she's dead.'

'That's not surprising –' began Dónal O'Leary.

The magpie interrupted by shouting, 'It's bad for business to have anybody die on your premises, never mind meet their death by drowning in your well.'

'You're right,' said the pub owner. He turned to Dónal O'Leary. 'Would you take twenty pieces of silver and promise me you'll never tell anyone about how your mother died?'

'B-b-b –' said Dónal O'Leary.

'Dónal O'Leary,' shouted the magpie, 'will you do as you're told and keep quiet about how your mother died if you're paid thirty pieces of gold and she's given a decent burial at the pub owner's expense.'

'That's too much,' complained the pub owner.

'No, it's not!' said the magpie firmly. 'Those are the terms. Take them or leave them and remember it's your livelihood that's at stake.'

The pub owner thought about it for a minute, then said, 'Agreed.'

'Agreed,' said Dónal O'Leary.

So Dónal O'Leary went home with thirty pieces of gold. He sat down by the fire and counted them. He could hardly believe his luck so he counted them again. He took out the thirty pieces of silver and began to count them too, then he began to laugh and laugh and laugh. He laughed so long and so hard Hutton and Dutton came to see what was going on.

'Why are you laughing?' they asked.

'I'm happy! It's like this,' said Dónal O'Leary. 'I don't know what happened to old Mother last night. She appeared happy and well before she went to bed but when I woke up she was dead.

'I was very upset, then I began to count my blessings. She was a good woman so she'll go straight to heaven. She was rich when she died. She had a long life and was happy and I could afford to give her a decent burial.

'I decided to do the best I could for her so carried her body into town to arrange for a lovely funeral and do you know dead women are in great demand? There's a war on and their bones are needed to make gunpowder. I sold her corpse for thirty pieces of gold.'

'We don't believe you,' said Hutton and Dutton.

'I don't care if you believe me or not,' said Dónal O'Leary. 'I've got the money and that's all I care about. If I didn't get the money for her body where else would I get it?'

Hutton and Dutton went home in a rage.

'It doesn't matter what happens to Dónal O'Leary,' snarled Hutton. 'He could fall into a dung heap and come out smelling of roses. It's not fair.'

'We should have killed our old mother instead of his,' complained Dutton. 'Let's kill her now, go into town and sell her body. She's a waste of space. She does nothing but eat and drink.'

'Good idea,' said Dutton.

So Hutton and Dutton killed their old mother, took her body into town and tried to sell it. They carried her on their backs as they shouted, 'Old woman's body for sale! Fine bundle of bones! Would make great gunpowder! Old woman's body for sale! For sale! Old woman's body!'

The townspeople were disgusted.

'Fancy that!' they exclaimed. 'Imagine trying to sell an old woman's body. They should be ashamed of themselves. They should bury her.'

So Hutton and Dutton were forced to bury their old mother. They were raging!

'That's the straw that broke the camel's back,' they complained. 'We have had enough! Let's go home, kidnap Dónal O'Leary and kill him.'

They rushed back to Dónal O'Leary.

'You,' they said, 'are for the chop.'

'Why?' asked Dónal O'Leary. 'What have I done?'

'You said you sold your old mother for thirty pieces of gold. You must have been telling lies. We couldn't sell our old mother.'

'I showed you the money I got. It's not my fault if the market's been saturated since yesterday,' protested Dónal O'Leary.

'That's beside the point,' snarled Hutton and Dutton. 'You're for the chop. We are sick, sore and tired at the sight of you. We're going to throw you in the river, that's what. That'll larn you!'

They grabbed Dónal O'Leary, shoved him in a large bag, tied the top securely and set off towards the river. They passed the pub on the way. It was a hot day and they felt thirsty so they put the sack against the wall and went inside.

Dónal O'Leary was very uncomfortable inside the sack. He moved around and tried to free himself. The sack was firmly tied so he couldn't get out. Then he began to think and think and think.

'I've had a good life,' he thought. 'I'm too young to die but that's not necessarily a bad thing. It means I'll get to heaven earlier than I expected. I'll see Daisy and my old mother again. Heaven's a beautiful place, much nicer than earth. I should be happy I'm going there.'

The more he thought about heaven the happier he felt so he began to sing hymns such as 'Jesus wants me for a sunbeam' and 'I'm H-A-P-P-Y' when along the road came a miserable rich man. He was so wealthy he had twenty-four cows. In today's terms that would mean he was a millionaire. He had no sense. Instead of being happy because he had so much money he was sad because he felt he might lose it. He was surprised and curious when he heard singing coming from the sack beside the pub door so he opened it and looked inside.

'Hello' said Dónal O'Leary.

'Hello' said the miserable man. 'What are you doing in there and why are you singing?'

'I'm sitting here singing because I'm happy I'm going to heaven.'

'Can I get in beside you and go to heaven too?' asked the miserable man.

'Sorry,' said Dónal O'Leary, 'there isn't enough room for you.'

'Well, will you change places with me?' asked the miserable man.

'No!' said Dónal O'Leary. 'I can't wait to get to heaven. Why should I let you have my place?'

'Would you swap places with me if I gave you all my cows?'

'What cows?' asked Dónal O'Leary.

'All those cows I have with me. Look behind me and see for yourself.'

So Dónal O'Leary peeped out of the sack and saw the cows. They were very fine animals.

'In that case,' said Dónal O'Leary, 'heaven can wait as far as I'm concerned. I'll let you have my place.'

He climbed out of the sack and the miserable man climbed in. Dónal O'Leary tied the sack securely. He had just enough time to drive the cows round a bend in the road so Hutton and Dutton didn't see them when they came out of the pub. Hutton and Dutton picked the sack up, carried it to the river and threw it in. The miserable man drowned. He was put out of his misery, but nobody knows whether he went to heaven or not.

The twins were happy as they returned home.

'That's that!' gloated Hutton.

'Yes,' Dutton agreed. 'That's fixed Dónal O'Leary. He'll never be able to bother us again.'

You can imagine how upset they were when they saw Dónal O'Leary singing as he walked beside his cows in his field. They rushed over to him.

'How did you get out of the sack?' asked Hutton.

'It burst open under the water and I swam out.'

'And where did you get those beautiful cows?'

'You're never going to believe me so I'm not going to tell you.'

'TELL US,' shouted Hutton and Dutton grabbing Dónal O'Leary by the throat and threatening to strangle him.

'Well, as you put it that way, I'll tell you. You're not going to believe me, but there are hundreds of cows living at the bottom of the river. I could only manage to bring twenty-four home so I think I'll go back again tomorrow and collect a few more.'

'WE DON'T BELIEVE YOU!' shouted Hutton and Dutton.

'I told you you wouldn't believe me,' said Dónal O'Leary, 'but if I'm not telling the truth, explain where I got all these cows.'

Hutton and Dutton thought about it for a minute.

'Show us where you got those cows,' demanded Hutton and Dutton.

'No!' replied Dónal O'Leary. 'Why should I tell you?'

'Because we'll choke you if you don't.'

'Well, seeing as how you put it that way, I'll show you,' replied Dónal O'Leary.

He took Hutton and Dutton down to the riverbank.

'There,' he said, 'do you see that part of the river where the water's very, very deep. That's where the cows are. Why don't you jump in and collect them?'

Hutton took a big buck leap and landed in the middle of the deepest part of the river.

Dutton and Dónal O'Leary watched as he sank under the surface. Bubbles rose up, Hutton surfaced, raised an arm above the water and shouted, 'Help!'

Dónal O'Leary turned to Dutton and said, 'There! You can see I was telling the truth. Your brother wants you to help him herd cows.'

Dutton ran towards the river and jumped.

Hutton and Dutton were never seen again.

Dónal O'Leary went home and lived a prosperous, happy, contented life.

21

THE MOUNTAIN DEW
(POTEEN)

*I am grateful to my old friend Ernie Scott and to local historians
Pat Cassidy and Viki Herbert from Lisnaskea for information and
stories about the mountain dew, also known as poteen, the cratur
or Irish whiskey. Both men are now gone but the memory of
their laughter lingers on. Thankfully Viki is still with us.*

The late Pat Cassidy was tall and thin with a laughter-crinkled face.
He told me, with a smile, that in the past making and selling poteen,
also called 'mountain dew', was the mainstay of the Fermanagh
economy. Of course such activities were highly illegal and there were
severe penalties if you were caught. He chuckled as he said, 'It was a
game, a serious game, but a game nevertheless. The Irish aren't stupid
and that's particularly true of Fermanagh men. We understand the
law very well. We just ignore it when need be.

'The law's an ass. How do the government expect people to
survive by farming poor-quality soil in the mountains? Be legal,
grow grain, take your grain to market and you get a pittance for it.
Ye could nae live on it at all, at all, at all. But turn that same grain
into mountain dew and that's a different story! Poor crops mean
the only means of survival is by selling poteen. Two stones of grain
would sell for about 1s 6d, if you were lucky. A gallon of poteen
made from the same amount of grain would sell for about 4s 6d.
And the leavings will fatten your cow. That's particularly good in

a district where grazing, or hay, is hard to come by. I've seen many revenue men sniffing about in the mountains when a sleek fat cow walked past him. Any fool'd know you can't fatten a cow on the heather but the revenue men can't prove nothing nohow! They're rightly flummoxed! Anyone with a titter of wit would know you couldn't fatten a gander on three acres of heather-covered mountain. You know the old saying, "Gold under furze, silver under grass and hunger under heather." Fermanagh's mountains are covered in heather.'

Pat told me stills, as well as being hidden in the mountains and glens, were often kept on small, remote uninhabited islands in Lough Erne. He said he learnt to row his cot backwards so that anyone watching would think he was coming when he was going.

I asked what a 'cot' was and he explained it's a special type of boat used in Fermanagh. It is the only boat in the world that is scuttled annually to preserve it.

Pat also told me stills were often hidden in mountain bogs.

'Wasn't that dangerous?' I asked. 'Couldn't you get lost in a bog, fall in, be sucked under the surface and drown?'

Pat laughed heartily at the idea.

'You could,' he replied, 'but don't forget we're locals. We know the countryside like the back of our hands. It's different for the revenue men. They're just blow-ins. They're not well acquainted with the landscape and they're scared of the bogs. They'll always travel on well-marked paths. Locals are different. They'll take the makings of a still out to the bogs in bits and pieces so nothing can be pinned on them. They'll put it all together on-site. If you've a still out in the bogs, a couple of dogs and a horse, you're landed.'

'Why do you need a couple of dogs and a horse to make whiskey?'

'If a mist comes down unexpectedly a horse can always find its way home. It can be cold and damp out distilling whiskey and sure any mortal man needs a wee nip of the cratur to warm the cockles of his heart. If you imbibe a bit much and have difficulty mounting your horse all you did was grab the hault of its tail and let it lead you home.'

'And what about the dogs?'

'If you're stuck in the bogs all night you can get very, very cold and go into the type of sleep from which you never wake up. Dogs are great at keeping a man warm. Many's the time I've dozed with a dog lying on my chest and another wrapped round my head. Warm as toast I was. And I'm still alive to tell the tale!'

Pat said he'd a friend who visited a site on the mountains where poteen was being brewed. It was a freezing cold night and a mist came down. The man became frightened because he couldn't find his way home. He was afraid of sinking into a bog hole, never to be seen again. He lay down with his black-and-white collie dog and the heat from the dog's body kept him from dying from exposure.

Pat said he knew a tramp who always slept outside and asked him how he kept warm. The tramp replied, 'I lie down on stones. They are heated by the sun during the day. At night that heat is transferred to my body. I'm fine as long as I have a dog to cover my feet.'

In the past, few people had shoes and a dog would have been a comfort on cold, bare feet.

According to Pat, poteen was originally made from barley. That makes the best whiskey of all. However, the stiller runs a high risk of being caught because barley needs to be spread out and given plenty of space to germinate and then dry. The amount of space required could easily be spotted by the forces of law and order, so a serious change had to be made in the manufacturing process. Stillers turned to water, sugar and yeast. It's impossible to arrest anyone because he has these substances. They are common in every household.

Sugar was rationed during the Second World War. This caused a shortfall in the production of poteen until the stillers started to use tins of syrup. Pat laughed heartily and said, 'A friend of mine was taken to court because the revenue men found he had a suspicious number of empty syrup tins. He pleaded "Not Guilty" and when

'Ye're kidding? Do ye mean to say
yer master expects you to keep
him alive in the bogs at night?'

asked to explain why he had so many empty tins of syrup on his premises he replied, "If it please your Honour, it's not illegal to like syrup."

'He was acquitted.'

Fermentation is the first process that takes place during the manufacture of poteen. The yeast becomes active and begins to grow. At first it feeds on sugar, water, germinated barley and anything else the stiller has put into his container. It, like us, breathes in oxygen and gives off carbon dioxide, which comes out of the wash as bubbles. The yeast grows quickly and uses up all the oxygen in its container. This is the point at which fermentation begins to take place, with alcohol being produced as a by-product. Unfortunately for the yeast it is killed when the alcohol content reaches around 17 per cent and fermentation stops. The next stage involves making the alcohol more concentrated by distilling the wash to form a whiskey.

Pat said fermentation occurred quickly outside in warm weather but slowed down, or stopped, when the weather grew cold. He frequently met 'poteen' men sneaking out furtively to their hidden places, in bogs, on islands or in the mountains, with hot water bottles and some extra sugar hidden in their coats. The hot water bottles were packed around their containers to raise the temperature and the sugar was used to give the contents 'a wee bit of a boost'.

Some women made poteen using a kettle. Pat said he was curious about how this was done because he thought a normal kettle would be inefficient. The spout's too near the liquid to let the alcohol escape. Eventually he met a woman who said she made poteen in a kettle. He asked her how she did it and she said, 'I had a large kettle specially made with a spout at the top instead of down the side. It provides enough space to allow the alcohol to come off efficiently. I put plates in a bucket of cold water, which I keep beside me to make them cold and I have a basin. I take one plate at a time out of the bucket, dry it and hold it over the spout of the kettle. The alcohol forms on the plate and I have a basin underneath to collect it.

'That's a great way to make poteen because I set the yeast and sugar to ferment in an innocent-looking jar in a cupboard. It looks as if I'm making wine. The cupboard and jar are clean so they're unlikely to become contaminated. The fermentation takes place quickly in the heat so I am guaranteed to produce good poteen. Every household has a kettle, sugar and yeast. I can't be arrested because I don't have any suspicious-looking apparatus. And what revenue man in his right mind would bother looking twice at a woman working by a fire with a kettle and some plates?'

According to Pat a lot of poteen produced in the past could be poisonous because unscrupulous stillers threw anything they had around into their brew – potato skins, beetroot, methylated spirits. They were frightened of being caught, so they produced an alcoholic brew in the shortest time possible. The shorter the time, the less likely the revenue men were to catch them and put them on trial. If convicted, they could be given a jail sentence. The best poteen came from those who made some for their own use and had a few bottles spare, which they could either sell or give away. They sometimes added beetroot to their 'good' poteen because it gave a pleasant taste and colour. Stillers who used methylated spirits frequently cut corners. They were not fussy about hygiene and as a result people who drank it could become ill.

My old friend Ernest Scott told me about making poteen near Ballynure in County Antrim. He said a friend of his was busy with the third distillation when he got word the revenue men were coming. Immediately he threw the poteen, still and all, into his duck pond. The trouble was the poteen was very strong, the pond was very small and the ducks became drunk! They started staggering around, quacking loudly, tripping over their feet and trying to fly. One of the revenue men was nearly hit by a low-flying duck.

'Was there more or less poteen made in Fermanagh than in the rest of Ulster?' I asked.

Pat replied, 'The roads in Fermanagh are poor. That's a great advantage. The revenue men are unlikely to travel up bad, remote roads, so there was more distilling here than in counties Down and Antrim, where the roads are good.'

Country folk had, and perhaps still have, a conviction that the law's an ass trying to keep them from making an honest living by turning their own hard work into a product they could sell. Ulster had the largest proportion of small farms in Ireland – that is, farms under five acres in size – and they were rack-rented almost out of existence. As Pat Cassidy, said, 'People have to live.'

The stillers thought any means of putting revenue off their scent was jus-tified. Many officers of the law were delayed, kidnapped or led astray. If the moon was in the right quarter and the grain was ripe the stillers would stage a mock faction fight to divert police attention. If the stillers were in danger of being discovered the still would be taken apart by a fast runner and carried across moun-tain roads. He'd be relieved by another runner, who would be relieved by a third and so on. By morning the still would be at the far side of the country and the police would have no evidence of a crime having been committed.

In the nineteenth century, Head Constable John Mullarchy reported, 'If there is an outrage against life or property we would get information from the respectable portion of the community; but as regards illicit distill-ing we get no advice; they take it as a matter of course. They do not con-sider it a moral offence.'

Even when the police managed to find poteen the struggle with the stillers was not over. A story has been preserved by folklore about three revenue officers who found a small

'No! I won't touch poteen! It's illegal!'

keg of poteen hidden in a farm outhouse. The farmer and his sons had disappeared so they carried the keg down to the nearest village. Everybody there seemed to be willing to help them, but nobody actually did. The police were told the local hackney driver had gone 'to a funeral, or it might be a wedding, with his long car'. They were very, very sorry, but nobody knew where the 'funeral' or 'wedding' was. There was no transport so the officers could not leave. They had no option but to take a room for the night in the local tavern. They didn't want to take any chances with their find so they carried the keg up to their bedroom and asked for a meal to be served there. Once the officers were upstairs a serious, whispered conversation was held with the waitress. Money exchanged hands. She carried the food upstairs, came down and said, 'It's between the fire cheek and the door, three boards out from the wall.'

The stillers used a belly brace to bore a hole through the ceiling, the floorboards and the bottom of the keg, then they drained the poteen off into a bucket. The policemen were left without any evidence whatsoever!

The distillation process needs to be well hidden to avoid detection. Boiling wash has a distinctive smell which betrays the fact that distilling is taking place. Stillers sometimes burnt bog fir, tarred boards or tyres to disguise the scent.

Special courses were run for the police in their barracks where they smelt and tasted all types of liquors. (That sounds as if it could have been fun!)

Viki Herbert, who lives in Lisnaskea, recounts being told the following story from the not so distant past by Jim Graham, who used to live and work on Crom Estate.

The head gardener, Mr Hislop, was a straight-laced, honest man. He was regarded with such respect he was always referred to as 'mister'. He was responsible for selling excess estate produce in the local markets. The soil was rich and well cared for so crops were plentiful. Mr Hislop did not like to sell substandard produce so the gardeners used to share lopsided or odd-shaped fruit and vegetables with their neighbours. Tom

Bailey, one of the neighbours, went to thank the gardeners with a wee bottle of the cratur. Mr Hislop refused to touch it because it was illegal.

'If I brought you a bottle of whiskey, would you drink that?' asked Tom.

'Sure I would,' came the swift reply.

So Tom went home, got an empty whiskey bottle, half-filled it with poteen and topped it up with cold tea. The next morning he took it back to Mr Hislop, who enjoyed it greatly.

Some years ago I hosted two storytellers from South Carolina. I took them to visit a traditional fiddler and the three of them were instant friends. They were drinking poteen within minutes.

The following night I took them to a storytelling session and a friend said he'd take them to his house after the session because he had some old books he'd like to show them. He promised to bring them back to my house when they'd finished. I was tired and went home to bed. My guests staggered in at about three o'clock in the morning after a great time drinking out of hours in a local pub. They were delighted because they'd been given more poteen.

'Don't you realise?' I asked, 'You've been in this country for less than forty-eight hours and you've already broken the law twice.'

They laughed and said, 'We love it here! People won't obey the law unless they think it's sensible! What harm did we do sitting, having a wee dram and a bit of *craic* until the wee hours of the morning?

'We were told that poteen's the liquor of life. It's a kind of a cure-all. It's what you give a sick calf or rub on your joints if you've got rheumatism or arthritis. You can mix it with hot water and a spoonful of sugar and the juice of a lemon to cure colds and flu. Sure, it was introduced into Ireland by St Patrick himself and was produced by monks in monasteries mainly for medicinal purposes. We're jet-lagged. We need a bit of life breathed into us!

'The word poteen comes from '*pota*'. That's the Gaelic word for small pot. Leprechauns used to make poteen in a small pot. We think that small pot is the gold you find at the end of a rainbow. It's magic. Surely you don't think two stray Americans should be denied a bit of Irish magic?'

22

THE REMARKABLE ROCKET

This is one of Oscar Wilde's stories. I have included it because Oscar Wilde was educated, as a boarder, in Portora Royal School, Enniskillen. I am indebted to my good friend Sheila Lahiffe, who, many years ago, arranged for me to stay at her family home in Dublin. There I had what Americans refer to as 'a blast'. We exchanged stories and Sheila's sister, Mary, gave me a book of fairy tales by Oscar Wilde. I was entranced by it and have been a fan of Oscar Wilde ever since. I have retold this tales in my own words. It is a story with a moral, although he himself wrote, 'It is a very dangerous thing to tell a story with a moral'!

The whole country was in an uproar and everyone was excited. Their prince, who was tall and handsome with hair like fine gold and large, dreamy, violet eyes, was getting married. It was like a fairy tale. His fiancée came from Finland. These were the days when it was part of the Russian Empire. She arrived in Ireland in a beautiful sledge shaped like a lovely golden swan. She lay on white silken cushions between the swan's folded wings. The sledge was drawn by six reindeer and she wore a soft white ermine cloak that reached right down to her tiny feet and a tiny cap made of silver tissue on her head. Her skin was as white as snow. Of course people in Ireland don't see snow often and if they do, it usually doesn't stay around for long so they said, 'The princess is beautiful. She is just like a white rose.'

When the prince saw the princess he fell immediately in love.

'Your picture was beautiful,' he said, 'but you are ten times more beautiful!'

The princess lowered her eyes modestly and blushed.

A young page boy standing beside her said, 'She was like a white rose, but now she's like a red rose.'

The whole court was delighted and so was the king. Everybody went around saying, 'Red rose, white rose, white rose, red rose.'

'That page boy has a lot of sense,' said the king. 'Double his wages.'

As the page boy was never given any wages, that made no difference to him at all, but everyone in the court said, 'What an honour for the page boy! His wages have been doubled.' And the page boy was delighted to know he'd been honoured.

The marriage ceremony was magnificent. The bride and groom walked hand-in-hand up the aisle together under a purple velvet canopy embroidered with little pearls. They were so happy and so much in love they could hardly keep their eyes off each other.

After the ceremony the prince and princess sat in the middle of the top table and drank out of a crystal loving cup.

'Ahhhhhh,' said the court. 'See how much they love each other. The cup has stayed as clear as glass. If false lips touch it, it turns cloudy.'

The wedding breakfast lasted five hours, after which there was a ball. The bride and groom danced the rose dance together and the king was so pleased he played his flute. He was a terrible flute player. He didn't have one note of music in his head. He only knew two tunes. He kept forgetting which tune he was playing and getting mixed up. He made a terrible squeaky noise but he didn't know that. He was the king so nobody dared tell him.

It was dark when the ball ended and everybody went outside to watch the firework display. The little princess was very excited. She'd never seen fireworks. The king ordered the royal pyrotechnist to be in attendance in case anything went wrong.

The princess turned to the prince and asked, 'What are fireworks like?'

'They are like the Aurora Borealis,' replied the king, who always answered questions meant for other people. 'They light up the sky.

Frankly I prefer fireworks to stars because you know when they are going to appear. You are in for a treat, my dear, because fireworks are as delightful as my flute-playing.'

A great stand had been put up at the end of the king's garden and as soon as the royal pyrotechnist had put everything in place the fireworks began to talk to one another.

'Oh look!' cried a little squib. 'What a beautiful garden. Just look at all those yellow tulips. They're gorgeous. I'm so glad I've had the opportunity to travel. Travel improves the mind and does away with prejudices.'

'You stupid squib,' sneered the big Roman candle. 'The king's garden is not the whole world. The world is an enormous place. It takes at least three days to see it properly.'

The Catherine wheel had been attached to an old deal box when she was young and had suffered from a broken heart,

'The world is any place you love,' she said sadly. 'Unfortunately poets have written so much about love they've killed it. Nobody believes in it any more. And I don't blame them. True love suffers and is silent. Romance is dead.'

'Feel your head,' said the Roman candle. 'Love and romance never dies. They go on for ever, like the sun, the moon and the stars. The prince and princess are truly in love. That love will be everlasting. I heard it from the brown paper I shared a drawer with. He knew all the latest court news.'

The Catherine wheel was one of those sad people who think if you repeat something over and over it eventually comes true, so she shook her head.

'Romance is dead. Romance is dead. Romance is dead,' she sighed.

A sharp dry cough was heard. Everyone looked round. It came from a tall, superior-looking, supercilious rocket. He was attached to the end of a very long stick. He always coughed before he spoke. He believed that attracted attention and added gravity to his words.

'Ahem! Ahem!' he said and all the fireworks stopped to listen – all, that is, except the poor Catherine wheel who was still shaking her head and murmuring, 'Romance is dead! Romance is dead!'

'Order! Order!' shouted a cracker because he thought that was the right thing to say. He wanted to be a politician and had studied parliamentary procedure.

'Quite dead,' whispered the Catherine Wheel before falling into a deep sleep.

As soon as there was perfect silence the rocket began to talk in a slow, distinguished manner.

'The king's son is very lucky to be married on the day I shall be let off. If it had been arranged beforehand it could not have been more fortunate for him, but then those of royal blood tend to be very lucky.'

'Oh dear me!' said the little squib. 'I thought it was the other way around and we were to be let off in honour of the prince's nuptials.'

'You are probably being let off to honour the prince and his charming princess, but I – I am different. I am quite remarkable. My mother was a famous Catherine wheel. She was three feet across and danced quite beautifully, achieving nineteen pirouettes before she eventually went out. Each time she turned she threw seven pink stars into the air. She was made of the best of gunpowder.

'My father was of French extraction and a rocket like myself. He flew so high people thought he would never come down again. He was a kindly being so when he saw all those anxious faces looking up into the sky he decided not to worry them and descend. He made a stupendous descent in a shower of golden rain. The press wrote about him in very flattering terms and the *Court Gazette* said he was "a triumph of Pylotechnic Art".'

'"Pyrotechnic Art" is the correct term,' said a Bengal light. 'I saw it written on my canister.'

'I said "Pyrotechnic",' said the rocket in a very cross tone of voice. 'I am never wrong so you should know not to contradict me. It is extremely bad manners to contradict. You should know better.'

The Bengal light felt put down so began to bully the little squibs to show he was still a person of some importance and a force to be reckoned with.

'As I was saying,' continued the rocket. 'As I was saying … What was I saying?'

'You were talking about yourself,' replied the Roman candle.

'So I was. I knew I was talking about something very interesting. I always find conversations about me extremely interesting, don't you?'

The Catherine wheel began to snore.

'Just listen to that,' complained the rocket. 'I'm being interrupted yet again. I hate being interrupted. It gets on my nerves as I'm a very sensitive, highly strung soul.'

The cracker turned to the Roman candle and whispered, 'What's a sensitive person?'

The Roman candle bent over the little cracker and whispered in her ear, 'A person who because he's got corns himself goes and treads on other people's toes!'

The little cracker couldn't help it. She laughed and laughed and laughed.

'Pray, what are you laughing about?' asked the rocket, who was annoyed.

'I'm laughing because I'm happy,' smiled the little cracker.

'Happy! Happy!' exclaimed the rocket. 'You've no right to be happy. It's very selfish to be happy. You should be thinking about others. You should be thinking about me, the remarkable rocket. I'm always thinking about me and I expect everyone else to do so too. That is called sympathy. It's a virtue I possess to a high degree. Think, for instance, what a tragedy it would be if something happened to me so I did not go off tonight. The prince would never be happy again. Neither would the princess. Their whole married life would be ruined. As for the king, he would never get over it. In fact when I think about the possibility of that situation I am moved to tears.'

'If you want to go off tonight you'd better keep your gunpowder dry,' said the Roman candle.

'That's right,' said the Bengal light, who had recovered his sense of self-esteem and was feeling better.

'Common sense!' sneered the rocket. 'You forget I am a very remarkable rocket, very remarkable and very uncommon. Anyone can exhibit common sense, if they haven't any imagination. I on the other hand have been gifted with a vivid imagination. I never think of things as they are. I always view them in a different light. As for keeping myself dry! Huh! You obviously do not appreciate my emotional nature. It is fortunate I could not care less. I am sustained by my sense of superiority. I have a big heart. None of you lesser mortals have hearts. Here you are, laughing and feeling happy when the prince and princess have just been married. What foolishness!'

'Why can't we be happy?' exclaimed a small fire balloon. 'It is a very happy event. The young couple love each other. Their hearts are full of joy. When I soar up in the air tonight I'm going to tell the moon and the stars all about it. You'll see them twinkle with happiness when they hear about our beautiful bride.'

'What a trivial view of life,' sniffed the rocket. 'If that's all that can be expected from you, you must be hollow and empty. Don't you realise the prince and princess could go and live in a far-off country and have a beautiful little son, with violet eyes and spun gold hair like his father. That poor little boy could be drowned in a river. What would you feel then? It doesn't bear thinking about. The thought is too dreadful to contemplate. The loss of their only son. I'll never get over that.'

'But they're only just married,' protested the fire balloon. 'They haven't had time to have a son, never mind lose one. They are happy. Nothing bad has happened to them.'

'I never said they had a son,' replied the rocket. 'I just said they might have one and they might lose him. If they did lose a son there would be no point in talking about it. I hate people who cry. The thought of their loss has me very much affected.'

'You are very affected,' said the Bengal light. 'In fact you are the most affected person I've ever known.'

'And you are the rudest person I've ever met,' replied the rocket. 'Understanding my friendship with the prince is quite beyond you.'

'But you don't even know him!' growled the Roman candle, who was beginning to feel annoyed.

'I never said I knew him. If I knew him I probably would not be able to be his friend. It is a very dangerous thing to know your friends.'

'The important thing is to keep yourself dry,' said fire balloon, who was very sensible.

'That may be important for you,' sniffed the rocket. 'But I shall weep if I so choose.'

He burst into tears, which flowed down his cheeks, along his chin, down his body and along his long stick to the ground, where it nearly drowned two little beetles, who were thinking of setting up home together and starting a family.

'You must be very romantic,' sighed the Catherine wheel, 'because you cry when there's nothing to cry about.'

The Roman candle and the Bengal light were annoyed and shouted, 'Humbug! Humbug! Humbug!' They were very practical people who, whenever they objected to anything shouted 'Humbug!'

It was a beautiful evening. The moon appeared to be smiling and it shone in the sky like a huge silver shield. The stars twinkled with joy, the air became scented by evening primroses and white lilies. Music sounded from the palace and the prince and princess danced beautifully together. The flowers stood on their tiptoes and peeped in through the windows while nodding their heads in time to the music.

Ten o'clock struck, then eleven, then on the stroke of midnight all of the courtiers came out onto the terrace.

'Let the firework display commence,' ordered the king.

The royal pyrotechnist bowed low, called for his six attendants, who each carried a flaming torch at the end of a long pole.

The effect was magnificent.

'Whizz! Whizz! Whizz!' went the Catherine wheel as the little rockets danced around. 'Boom! Boom! Boom!' went the Roman candle. The Bengal light made everything look scarlet, the Fire Balloon cried, 'Cheerioooooo!', as he soared upwards, dropping tiny blue sparks as he went. 'Bang! Bang! Bang!' went the crackers, who enjoyed themselves immensely. Everyone had a great time except the rocket. His gunpowder was so wet with his tears he could not go off. His poor relations, to whom he'd never speak without sneering, shot up into the sky, making wonderful showers of golden fire, and he just sat there, looking more supercilious than ever.

'I must be reserved for some really grand occasion. Perhaps the birth of an heir to the throne?'

The next day the workmen came to tidy up. The rocket felt pleased.

'This must be a deputation. I will receive them with the dignity becoming my station.'

'I knew I'd cause a sensation.'

He looked more superior than ever, stuck his nose in the air and frowned to give the impression he was thinking about something very serious. The workmen took no notice until they were going away, when one of them caught sight of him.

'Look at this!' he cried. 'Here's a bad rocket.'

He threw the rocket over the wall into a muddy ditch.

'BAD ROCKET? BAD ROCKET?' said the rocket as he whisked through the air. 'That's not what the man said. That's impossible! He must have said "GRAND ROCKET". "BAD" and "GRAND" sound very much the same. In fact they often are the same.'

He fell head first into the mud.

'This is very uncomfortable,' he said. 'It must be some fashionable watering place. A spa, that's what it is. I've heard fashionable people talking about going to a spa to help their nerves and goodness knows what. Considering the company I've been forced to keep I could do with a relaxing break. My nerves are completely shot to pieces. I have been placed upside down to reverse the effect of gravity on my brain. That should do me a power of good.'

A little frog, with a green mottled coat and bright intelligent eyes, hopped over to him.

'Hello,' he said, 'and welcome. I see you're enjoying a mud bath. There's nothing quite like mud. It's good for the blood, you know.'

'Ahem! Ahem!' coughed the rocket.

'What a wonderful singing voice you have,' exclaimed the frog. 'It's very like a frog's croak. Will you join us at our glee club tonight? We make the most musical sound in the world. The club's held in the duck pond near the farmer's house. We begin when the moon rises. The sound we make's so entrancing everybody stays awake to listen. Why only yesterday I heard the farmer's wife say she couldn't get a wink of sleep because of us. It's wonderful to be so popular.'

'Ahem! Ahem!' said the rocket. He was annoyed because the frog spoke so quickly he couldn't get a word in edgeways.

'Yes! You have a wonderful voice,' said the frog. 'And I do hope you will come and join us tonight. Now I must go and look for my six beautiful daughters. I'm afraid the pike, who's a perfect monster, will make a meal of them. Goodbye! It's been a pleasure talking to you. I must say I've enjoyed our conversation.'

'Huh! Conversation indeed!' snarled the rocket. 'We did not have a conversation. You did all the talking.'

'I like to do all the talking,' replied the frog. 'It prevents arguments and saves time.'

'I like arguments,' said the rocket.

'Arguments are vulgar. Everyone in society knows that. Now I really must go. I see my daughters in the distance.'

And with that the little frog hopped away.

The rocket put his nose in the air and said in his usual supercilious fashion, 'You are an annoying, ill-bred person. It's very irritating to find somebody who talks about himself all the time when I want to talk about myself. That is sheer selfishness on your part. Selfishness is a detestable characteristic, especially when exhibited to one of my temperament. I have a sympathetic nature. You should follow my example. I am a very important person. Don't you realise that yesterday the prince and princess got married in my honour? Of course a provincial, like you, would know nothing about what goes on at court.'

A large, bright blue dragonfly was sitting on a nearby bush.

'There's no point in talking to him,' she said, 'because he has gone away.'

'Well, that's his problem. I am not going to stop talking to him simply because he has gone away. I like to hear myself talk. I am such an excellent conversationalist. I often have long conversations with myself and I am so clever sometimes I do not understand what I say.'

'Well, then you should lecture on philosophy,' said the dragon-fly as she spread her lovely, gauze wings and soared up into the sky.

'How foolish of her not to stay,' said the rocket as he sank a little deeper into the mud. 'She has wasted a marvellous opportunity to have her mind stimulated and improved by the brilliance of my thought. However, I don't care one iota. I understand that genius such as mine is rarely appreciated by the lower classes.'

After some time a large white duck, with yellow legs and webbed feet, came up to him. She was considered a great beauty in the duck world because of her waddle.

'Quack, quack, quack,' she said, 'you're a very peculiar shape. Were you born like that or did you suffer a serious accident?'

'You are obviously something of an ignoramus,' replied the rocket. 'My shape is considered to be most elegant in refined circles. However, I will excuse you. You obviously do not move in high society so have never been given the opportunity to know better. I can fly up into the air and come down in a shower of golden rain.'

'A fat lot of use that is,' said the duck. 'It would be different if you could do something useful, like plough a field or pull a cart like a donkey or even look after sheep like a collie dog.'

'My good creature,' said the rocket in his haughtiest tone of voice, 'I can see you're a person of the lower orders. A person in my exalted position is never useful. We have accomplishments and that is more than enough. I have no sympathy whatsoever with any kind of industry. I maintain work is something done by people who have nothing else to do.'

The duck had a peaceful nature. She never saw the point in arguing with anyone.

'I suppose we all have our own ideas and opinions,' she said. 'Anyway I hope you come to live here.'

'I will not!' cried the rocket. 'I find this a very tedious place to be. It lacks the attributes of both society and solitude. It is merely suburban. I shall probably go back to court where I will make a sensation.'

'I thought of entering public life,' remarked the duck. 'There are so many things that need to be reformed. I took the chair of a committee and we passed resolutions condemning everything we didn't like. It didn't have any effect that I could see, so I gave up in disgust and went back to domesticity.'

'I am made for public life,' said the rocket, 'and so are all my relatives. We excite attention wherever we appear. When I eventually go off I will be a magnificent sight. Domesticity distracts the mind from the higher things of life and causes one to age rapidly.'

'Ahhh!' sighed the duck, 'The higher things of life. How wonderful! That reminds me, I'm hungry. I must go and find something to eat. Quack! Quack! Quack!'

With that she waddled over to the stream.

'Come back! COME BACK!' yelled the rocket. 'I have a lot to say to you.'

The duck paid no attention and disappeared from sight.

The rocket murmured to himself, 'I'm glad she has gone. She had a very middle-class mind. I should be careful of the company I keep. I would not want to be contaminated by the middle classes.'

He sank further into the mud and began to think about the loneliness of genius.

Suddenly two little boys appeared. They ran down the bank carrying a kettle and some sticks.

The rocket thought they must be part of a deputation and looked dignified, which is particularly difficult when you're standing on your head.

'Oh look!' cried one of the little boys. 'An old stick. I wonder how it got here? It'll do for our fire.'

'OLD STICK! Impossible!' said the rocket. 'He must have said "GOLD STICK". That is a compliment. He must mistake me for one of the court dignitaries!'

The little boys lit the fire and stuck the rocket on top before lying down on the grass and closing their eyes.

The rocket was very damp so it took a long time to dry out. Eventually he went on fire and became very excited.

'I'm going off!' he cried as he made himself stiff and straight. 'I'll go higher than the sun, higher than the moon and away up past the stars. I shall go so high that –'

Fizz! Fizz! Fizz! Up he went! Straight into the air!

'Yippeeeeee!' he yelled. 'I could go on like this for ever and ever! What a great sensation! I am a great success.'

The sun was shining brightly and nobody saw him.

Then he felt a curious tingling sensation in every pore of his body.

'I'm going to explode,' he thought. 'I will make a great noise that will be the talk of the court for at least a year and I shall cover the world with stars.'

BANG! BANG! BANG! His gunpowder was tremendously loud but nobody heard it.

Swoosh! The stars inside him burst into the sky and cascaded towards earth in a cloud of golden rain.

And nobody saw them, not even the two little boys, who were still lying in the sun with their eyes shut. All that was left of the rocket was an old stick. It fell down to earth and hit a goose, who was taking his afternoon stroll along the riverbank.

'Goodness!' said the goose. 'It's raining sticks!'

'I knew I'd create a great sensation,' gasped the rocket as he went out.

23

THE GREAT FAMINE (1845-1847)

The six counties of Ulster, of which Fermanagh is one, have, and had, the largest percentage of small farms – that is farms of less than 5 acres – in the whole of Ireland. A cheap, easily grown source of food was needed. This was supplied by Sir Walter Raleigh. He brought the potato to Ireland during the late sixteenth century. It was quickly adopted by the Irish as their main food crop because it enabled a small piece of land to produce sufficient food to feed a family. Potatoes and buttermilk form a reasonably healthy diet. Potatoes contain a comparatively large amount of Vitamin E and increased potato consumption resulted in a rise in the birth rate. The land grew overcrowded and rents rose to astronomical levels. They were much higher than those in the rest of the UK. Crops other than potatoes had to be sold to pay the rent and poor people were left to exist on what was effectively a monoculture. This led to crops becoming vulnerable to potato blight.

Over time there was a series of potato crop failures, resulting in famine. The most catastrophic was known as the Great Hunger, which officially lasted from 1845-1847.

Many factors caused the effects of the Great Hunger to be so devastating. To begin with, Victorian attitudes regarding hardship were different to those of today. People believed that misfortune was a result of sin. If you sinned God was sure to punish you. You should be ashamed of yourself and it would be wrong to interfere with God by helping the sufferer. This attitude permeated society at the time and even the royal family was affected by it. Queen Victoria gave birth to a disabled son. She felt obliged to keep him hidden from public view because he would have spoilt her.

There were many good landlords who did their best to help their tenants but others did not. They were absentee landlords who didn't know what was going on and perhaps did not care. They simply wanted rents to support extravagant lifestyles. During the period when the government bought Indian corn for distribution to Ireland one shipload of food was imported to Ireland for every six shiploads that were exported. Food distribution was difficult because the transport system was undeveloped. Science was in its infancy, so the cause of disease was unknown. Water became polluted and rats and houseflies were prevalent, resulting in the spread of disease.

At the time of partition, when the south of Ireland split from the rest of the United Kingdom, the southern government collected oral stories concerning the Great Famine. The Northern Irish government failed to do so, leading to the erroneous belief that Northern Ireland was not affected. Newspapers of the time record the horrendous truth about what happened, as did many people, including Oscar Wilde's mother, Lady Wilde.

Lady Wilde wrote under the pen name Speranza, for The Nationalist magazine. If the authorities had been able to identify her she would have met the same fate as the editor of the magazine, another Protestant, John Mitchel, who was arrested, taken to Dublin for a trial, found guilty of treason and transported to the New World as a slave.

Thankfully other writers, such as William Carleton, have preserved folklore about the famine.

The late Dr Bill Crawford, who became my good friend when I worked in the Ulster Folk and Transport Museum, talked about attitudes to the Great Famine. He said many survivors felt guilty for one of two reasons – they had either behaved badly and prof-ited from the disaster, so they had good reason not to talk about it, or they felt guilty because they had survived when others had died. Their memory lives on in folk tales. There is the gombeen man, who collected rents and was used to frighten naughty children. 'Be good or the gombeen man will get you!' Other people suffered from a mental condition known as non-rational guilt. The same condition may be observed today in those who have survived either accidents or wars.

Bill also said that footprints left by the Great Famine may be found in the oral history of some families. Kate Orr, who is now the vice principal of Edenderry Primary School in Banbridge, told me of one such case. She was born on a farm near Enniskillen. As a child she often wondered why there were so many unoccupied dwellings around the site on which she lived. Her father told her that before the Great Famine all those houses on their farm had been occupied. After the famine there was only one family left. Her father said the others had either died of starvation and disease or emigrated. She was also told that all the straight roads in County Fermanagh and all the silly ones going nowhere and ending in bogs were built to give employment to the starving. The trouble with that kind of work was it was badly organised. The pay was poor and workers often did not get their wages for several months after the job was completed, so they died of starvation.

In 1841 the government set up a system of workhouses throughout the British Isles that were intended to home starving, poverty-stricken people. According to folklore, these so-called places of refuge were horrific. They were built to one design. Each workhouse contained four compartments. When families entered, they were separated, with men, women, boys and girls being housed in different compartments. In effect this meant that you were unlikely to see your loved ones again. The regime was harsh, the work hard, disease rife and the food was poor. The idea was to destroy personal identity by taking away all personal possessions and providing uniform, ill-fitting clothes in harsh fabrics. New entrants were scrubbed with carbolic soap and had their hair cut off. It was humiliating. Nevertheless, such was the state of the country that many peopled pleaded to be admitted. As the situation deteriorated workhouses became overcrowded, people were turned away and riots ensued. During the twentieth century most of the workhouses were demolished but part of the one in Lisnaskea survives. Attempts are being made by locals to raise sufficient funding to turn it into a museum, in spite of local folklore saying it is haunted by a black pig.

The old male dormitory was used to house a sewing factory called Watts and Stone. Operators there reported seeing a black pig's ghost running up and down the stairs. If anything ever went wrong in the factory operators would say, 'It was the pig that did it!'

In the past, before dogs came to Ireland, pigs filled their place. Pigs can be house-trained, taught to come when they are called and respond to other commands. This type of pig was referred to as 'an educated pig'. Many people kept educated pigs as pets and an educated pig had the run of the house. All animals had to justify their existence and that was true of an educated pig. It was required to sire offspring that were sold and the money raised was used to pay the rent. The ghost of the black pig that haunts the old site of part of the Lisnaskea workhouse must have been an educated pig because it haunts the inside of the building. Perhaps it's looking for its owner who died there?

This is probably completely off the point but there is another black pig associated with Fermanagh. The Black Pig's Dyke (sometimes known as 'The Worm Ditch') is the remains of a long double ditch that used to form an old frontier defence along the border of Ulster. It is thought to date back to pre-Christian times. Could the ghost of the black pig that gave its name to the Black Pig's Dyke be the one that wanders around Lisnaskea workhouse?

After Lisnaskea workhouse ceased to function as a workhouse part of it was demolished and the site was used for a housing estate. When they were digging the foundations for a new dwelling workmen found the skeletons of two adults and a child. They had not been properly buried. All construction stopped until a priest arrived to deliver the last rites.

'Hungry grass' is referred to in relation to these miserable deaths in folklore. People say that when walking through fields they have suddenly become weak and had to lie down. When that happens it is important not to close your eyes and go to sleep because you've stumbled upon hungry grass. It marks the spot where a famine victim died of starvation. If you stumble upon hungry grass you must get off it quickly. It will be a struggle but staying on it puts you at risk of dying. Once you move away from it you will feel well again. Local historian Vicki Herbert tells of a place between Belturbet and Newtownbutler known as 'Starvation Row'.

The Fear Gorta (Man of Hunger) is an emaciated phantom who wanders through the countryside, begging for food and alms during famines. Giving him food brings good luck; sending him away unfed is bad luck.

The following 'famine' story is known throughout Ireland but I have followed the example of those living in Fermanagh by giving it a local touch and setting it near Florencecourt.

A poor farmer lived near the gates of Florencecourt with his wife and his old blind mother. He, being a man, was upset because he was starving. His wife, being a woman, had her eyes on higher things than food! She was heartbroken because she desperately wanted a baby. She had been married several years and had not yet heard the patter of little feet. The old mother was of a practical disposition.

'I am old and useless,' she sobbed. 'I can't see. How is a body supposed to help around the house if she can't see? I am nothing but another mouth to feed, a burden on my dear son and his wife. These are hard times. If I could only see I could help my family and not be a hindrance.'

'Being hungry's depressing,' the farmer thought. 'Maybe if I could find something for us to eat my wife and mother would cheer up. It's worth a try.' So he fetched his bow and a quiver full of arrows and sneaked quietly into Florencecourt demesne. This was a dangerous thing to do. If any of the gamekeepers caught him he would be severely punished. He was cautious as he slid from tree to tree, looking for anything he could shoot and take home to fill his cooking pot. Eventually he came to a clearing. He hid in the undergrowth surrounding it and rested. After a time, a huge white stag came into the clearing, 'Good!' thought the farmer. 'If I can get that stag home it can be salted and we'll have meat to eat for months.' He salivated at the thought and lifted his bow.

'Please don't shoot me,' pleaded the stag.

'I don't want to kill you. I'm sorry but my family's starving and we need to eat something. Your body's big enough to keep us alive for months.'

'Have mercy. If you shoot me my family will die. My wife's just had a baby. It was difficult birth. She's not strong enough to find enough food for herself and our baby.'

'I'm really sorry,' said the farmer, 'but it looks as if one of our families is going to die and I don't want it to be mine. I agree that's probably selfish of me but it's how I feel.'

'Haven't you noticed what colour I am?' asked the stag.

'Of course I have. You're white, aren't you?'

'Yes, I'm a pure white stag and a handsome one at that,' said the stag, who was inclined to be vain. 'Don't you know that white stags are magical? I could grant you a wish. Don't you think being granted a wish would be better than eating me? If you kill me, salt my body and stick it up your chimney to preserve it you will have enough to eat for a few months when you could wish for food to feed your family for the rest of your lives.'

'That would make both my wife and my mother angry.'

'Why should they object to you bringing them food?'

'Well, it's like this,' said the farmer. 'My wife longs for a baby, while my mother's blind and wants to be able to see again. She longs for that more than anything else in the world. If I wish for food they would say I was selfish and they'd be annoyed.'

'Couldn't you give me three wishes, please?'

'I'm sorry. I can't do that. It's beyond my powers and the other world would be angry if I attempted to do more than I'm supposed to, but I'll tell you what,' said the stag. 'Go home and discuss the situation with your family. I promise I'll meet you here tomorrow at the same time. You can tell me what you want to do then – either make a wish or shoot me.'

'How do I know you're not just tricking me and that you'll come back?'

'Put me under a *geis*,' suggested the stag, 'then you'll know I have to come back or I'll be cursed by the other world.'

The farmer put the stag under a *geis*, returned home and told his wife and mother what had happened.

'What are you going to ask for?' asked the wife.

The farmer said he was hoping to ask for sufficient food to feed his family for the rest of their lives. His wife burst into tears and sobbed, 'How can you be so selfish? All you think of is food when you know my heart is breaking because I haven't got a baby!'

'And how can you think of your stomach when you know all I want is to be able to see again?' sobbed the old mother.

The farmer was worried. He couldn't sleep that night. He just lay and worried and worried, wondering how he could get something to eat and also please his wife and his mother. Just before dawn he had a marvellous idea. He knew how to use his one wish. As he got ready to meet the stag he refused to tell his wife and his mother his intentions. You must never tell anyone about a wish you are about to make. If you do it won't come true.

The farmer whistled a happy tune as he went to meet the stag. Can you guess what he said when he met the stag?

He said, 'I wish my mother could see my wife rocking our baby in a golden cradle!'

Oscar Wilde's mother, Lady Wilde, was so moved by the plight of famine victims that she wrote the following poem, one of many, under the pen name of Speranza.

If the authorities had managed to discover Speranza's identity she could have been deported for treason for daring to disagree with the government.

'A Supplication'

'De profundis clamavi ad te domine'
By our looks of mute despair,

By the sighs that rend the air,
from lips too faint to utter prayer,
Kyrie Eleison.

By our last groans of our dying,
Echoed by the cold wind's sighing
On the wayside as they're lying,
Kyrie Eleison.

Miserable outcasts we,
Pariahs of humanity,
Shunned by all where'er we flee,
Kyrie Eleison.

For our dead no bell is ringing,
Round their forms no shroud is clinging,
Save the rank grass newly springing,
Kyrie Eleison.

Golden harvests we are reaping,
With golden grains our barns heaping,
But for us our bread is weeping,
Kyrie Eleison.

Death-devoted in our home,
Sad we cross the salt sea's foam,
But death we bring where'er we roam,
Kyrie Eleison.

Whereso'er our steps are led,
They can track us by our dead,
Lying on their cold earth bed,
Kyrie Eleison.

We have sinned – in vain each warning –
Brother lived his brother scorning,

Now in ashes see us mourning,
Kyrie Eleison.

We have sinned, but holier zeal
May we Christian patriots feel,
Oh! for our dear country's weal,
Kyrie Eleison.

Let us lift our streaming eyes
To God's throne above the skies,
He will hear our anguished cries,
Kyrie Eleison.

Kneel beside me, oh! my brother,
Let us pray each with the other,
For Ireland, our mourning mother,
Kyrie Eleison.

(Lady Wilde, writing under the pen name Speranza)

This story about the effect the Great Famine had on a family living in Ballybenone has been transcribed, word for word, from Dr Henry Glassie's excellent book, *Passing the Time*. He was told the story by Michael Boyle. It is reproduced with Dr Glassie's kind permission.

There was a man named O'Brien.
He lived somewhere in Rossnadoney,
in the Point of Rossnadoney as they call it.
And he had a wife
and five children,
five young children.
And they hadn't a haet; there was no food,
there was no food,
and they were in a starving condition.
And he said he'd *fish;*

> he'd try to *fish* in the Arney River,
> that run along his land,
> that was convenient to his land.
> He said he'd *fish*,
> try and fish to see would he get a few fish to eat
> that'd keep them from dyin'.
> So he did; he went out this day
> and he caught seven fish.
> Well, he went out every day,
> well, for a good many days.
> And he caught seven fish every day.
> And one of the children died.
> And he caught six then.
> And he caught six *every day.*
> And the number went down to six.

'Aye, I heard that too, about the time of the Great Famine. That happened in Rossnadoney, the townland of Rossnadoney, along the Arney River there.

'Now that happened; it was told anyway.

'It came down from the Famine days.'

24

THE LAKE OF
THE FAIR WOMAN
(NEAR GARRISON)

A poor man and his beautiful wife lived with their much-loved baby in the district of Clogherbeg, which lies between Holywell, Boho and Garrison. The landscape is wild, desolate and haunted. It acts as a refuge for displaced people during times of war.

The land around Clogherberg is poor, which makes it difficult to eke out a living there. At the time Garrison was a small village with a barracks that was originally built by King William III after the battle of Augher. Shortly after King William won the Battle of the Boyne, a troop of soldiers was stationed at Garrison. They terrorised the countryside. One day several off-duty soldiers found the mud hut in which the young couple were living. The couple were terrified, panicked and ran for their lives. The soldiers caught up with the husband and slaughtered him on the spot. Fear lent wings to his wife's feet. Clutching her infant to her breast she ran and ran until she reached the edge of the lake. She glanced back and saw the soldiers were still following her. She was terrified of what they might do to her.

There is a large rock beside the lake. She struggled up to the top of it, stood erect and shouted, 'Unto Thee I commend my spirit', as she jumped.

The kindly waters accepted her body and that of her baby and she sank beneath its dark, still depths. From that day to this streams of blood-like fluid flow from the bowels of the rock. That is why it is known as the Bleeding Rock and the lake is described as 'The Lake of the Fair Woman' (*Loch na mBan Fionn*). The Bleeding Rock's exposed surface measures about 18 by 9 feet. It is situated partly on land and partly in the water.

25

FOLK CUSTOMS AND CHARMS

Life in the past was frightening because people, animals and crops could suddenly sicken and die for no apparent reason. Society didn't have the benefit of modern technology and scientific research. People lived their lives much closer to nature than they do today. They kept a constant lookout for changes in the weather and signs that would help them predict the future. This gave rise to superstitions and ideas based on observation that are preserved in folklore.

Good weather in Ireland, like in other places, frequently follows a sunset during which the sky turns red while bad weather is often proceeded by a red sky in the morning, hence the old rhyme:

Red sky at night,
Shepherd's delight.
Red sky in the morning,
Shepherd's warning.

There is also an old saying about magpies, who were supposed to be aligned with the devil.

One for sorrow,
Two for joy,
Three for a girl,
Four for a boy.

Five for silver,
Six for gold,
Seven for a secret never to be told.

If a fisherman saw one magpie as he set off on a fishing expedition he would worry because this was believed to be unlucky. Bad luck could be averted by greeting the bird, saying, 'Good morning, Mr Magpie.'

Perhaps there is some sense behind the old rhyme because if a storm looms one magpie of a pair stays at their nest while the other forages for food. Storms can put a fisherman's life at risk.

Folklore also has a way of forecasting future harvests by observing bees:

A swarm of bees in May
Is worth a load of hay,
A swarm of bees in June
Is worth a silver spoon.
A swarm of bees in July
Is not worth a fly.

In other words, if the weather is sufficiently good early in the season to enable bees to pollinate the crops, the harvest will be good. It will be poor if the weather is so inclement that the bees are unable to reproduce and swarm until July.

If frogs lay their eggs at the edge of the pond the weather's going to be cold and wet. If they place their frogspawn in the middle of the pond a warm summer can be expected. Warm weather causes water to evaporate, which could cause the pond to dry up. Frogspawn laid along the edge would die in such conditions. Conversely frogspawn laid at the edge of a pond in wet weather would not be in danger.

I thought that sounded logical until I met an old man in the post office in Brookeborough. We started chatting about the weather, agreeing that it was, as usual, 'diabolical'! He said it was going to be a wet summer and I replied, 'The frogs in my garden disagree. Their spawn is in the middle of my pond.' He turned and snarled.

'Them frogs know nothing!' He was right. It was a very wet summer and I was sadly disillusioned with the forecasting ability of frogs.

Rooks were also used to forecast the weather. If they place their nests high in the trees, folklore holds that it will be a good summer; if they built them on lower branches the weather will be poor. A plentiful supply of berries in autumn suggests a hard winter.

Another folk belief holds that if the first butterfly you see in spring is brown you will have to eat cheap brown bread for a year because you will be poverty-stricken and unable to afford expensive white bread. If the first butterfly you see is white it indicates a year of plenty, while a brightly coloured butterfly means great prosperity. Different types of butterflies hatch at different times of the year, according to the weather, so perhaps this is another piece of folklore based on accurate observation?

Butterflies were thought to be the souls of the dead. There is a sad story about a little girl who loved her grandfather very much. He died and she was sitting crying in the corner when a brightly coloured butterfly flew into the house. It attracted her attention. She got up and chased it. Her grandmother was extremely angry. 'Don't you realise that's your grandfather's soul?' she scolded. 'You shouldn't be chasing him. Leave him in peace.' The poor child was devastated to think she had upset her grandfather.

If a man has whooping cough he should walk until he meets a man on a white horse, then he should ask that man for a cure. He will be cured by whatever the rider tells him to eat. Another folk cure is to pass the patient over and under the belly of a donkey or to use a frog to strike the patient's mouth while he or she is coughing. There is no record of what effect that 'cure' had on the frog!

Another whooping cough cure is to put garlic in your shoes or socks so it is pressed against the skin of your feet. It sounds crazy, but there could be some sense behind it. Garlic penetrates the skin and enters the bloodstream so the breath smells of garlic within fifteen minutes of being applied to the feet. It has strong antiseptic properties and certainly won't do any harm.

People believed that if they bound their heads in ivy they could drink as much alcohol as they liked without becoming drunk!

'We can't be drunk!
We've tied ivy round
our heads.'

A traditional cure for a hangover was to bury the sufferer up to the neck in moist river sand.

Thomas Connor, who lived in Ederney, must have been as strong as a horse to survive the cure for common colds, which he practised each springtime in which a cut was made in a vein and blood was allowed to flow freely. Thomas was eighty-eight and still observing the old custom when his action was recorded by the late Jim McVeigh in 1940.

A seventh son is supposed to have the cure for evil while a seventh daughter has the cure for facial paralysis. Personally I'd like a definition of 'evil'!

Many people were reputed to have charms, which were passed down from generation to generation, to cure diseases. A charm for heart failure, for example, involved making the patient sit on a chair, then getting a glass of oatmeal and walking round the patient three times. Secret words were spoken and the glass was examined. Some of the meal would have disappeared. The amount left was thought to indicate the severity of the heart problem; the greater the amount in the glass, the more serious the disease. The remaining oatmeal was made into a cake, which was given to the affected person to eat. This charm could be repeated three times.

Some people were thought to 'over look' children, causing them a mild ailment, such as loosing their appetite or catching a cold. To prevent this, the mother would secretly pray, 'May every eye that sees you bless you' whenever anyone entered.

The reason we say, 'Bless you', when somebody sneezes is because of the old folk belief that when you sneeze your soul leaves your body for a split second and the devil could grab it. The blessing prevents this from happening.

If a blackberry cane was rooted at both ends, it was believed to have magical properties. Children were passed under blackberry arches to cure hernias.

There were some equally bizarre customs for getting rid of toothache, such as kneeling on any grave in any graveyard, saying three paters and three aves for the soul of the person lying underneath, then taking a handful of grass from the grave and giving it a good chew. You were supposed to spit each mouthful out. After all that it was believed you'd never suffer from toothache again.

There's a touch of the pagan to this next custom. You had to vow to God, the Virgin and the new moon that you'd never comb your hair on a Friday. After your toothache was cured you had to fall on your knees and say five prayers in gratitude, even if you were crossing a river at the time.

The following custom to get rid of toothache sounds more Christian in origin, but equally ineffective. You had to write out the following charm and sew it into your clothes.

> As Peter sat on a marble stone,
> The Lord came to him all alone.
> 'Peter, Peter, what makes you shake?'

> 'Oh Lord and Master, it is the toothache.'
> Then Christ said, 'Take these for my sake
> And never more you'll have toothache.'

Finally, to avoid a toothache altogether, you should never shave on a Sunday!

We may laugh, but toothache was once a serious disease, as well as being painful. During the sixteenth century it was the third most common cause of death.

26

THE FIDDLER'S MEMORIAL, CASTLE CALDWELL AND BELLEEK POTTERY

Thanks are due to Fergus Clery, Head of Design at Belleek Pottery, for telling me about the ghost that haunts Belleek Pottery.

Castle Caldwell railway station is near Belleek and about 12 miles from Bundoran in County Donegal. There is an unusual memorial nearby. It dates from the eighteenth century, is shaped like a fiddle and has the following words inscribed on it.

To the memory of James McCabe, who fell off St. Patrick's barge,
belonging to Sir James Caldwell Bart, and Count of Milan and
was drowned off this point August ye 13th, 1770:
"Beware ye fiddlers of ye fiddler's fate
Nor tempt ye deep lest ye repent too late
Ye have been deemed to water foes
Then shun ye lake till it with whiskey floes
On firm land only exercise your skill
There ye may play and drink your fill." D.D.D.

Around Castle Caldwell the three Ds are supposed to mean 'Denis Died Drunk'! However, it the more probable meaning is 'Drink Drowned Dennis'!

Denis McCabe was fiddler and jester to the Caldwell family and he was also what is locally known as 'a terrah for the drink'.

Sir James Caldwell owned many barges including one called the 'St Patrick'. He was a hospitable man who had many house guests. The barges were used by guests to sail on Lough Erne around Castle Caldwell. Those who did not want to go sailing lounged on terraces overlooking the lake.

Dennis usually sailed out on a barge and entertained the guests by playing his fiddle. He was drunk on the day he died. He got up to play his fiddle, staggered, fell overboard and drowned. All that can be said is that others on board must also have been well and truly inebriated or they would have managed to save the unfortunate fiddler.

Castle Caldwell has an interesting history. The founder of the Caldwell family in Ireland was born at Preston in Ayrshire. He was of planter stock and became a successful merchant in Enniskillen. When he died in 1639 his eldest son, James, settled at Rossbeg, afterwards called Castle Caldwell. James, like his father, was a man with both drive and ability. He was elected a baronet on 23 June 1863 and became High Sheriff of County Fermanagh in 1677. In local parlance he was 'some pup'!

As the Caldwell family were early settlers in Ireland, they belonged to the established Anglican Church. They moved away from Scotland before Presbyterianism became the common denomination so they remained Anglicans and were not affected by the Penal Laws. The Penal Laws were a series of laws passed over a long period of time that made life difficult for anyone who was not an Anglican, namely Presbyterians, Methodists and all other denominations of Protestantism, as well as Catholics. People belonging to these non-conformist religions were not allowed to be educated or join the armed forces and so on.

The Caldwell family must have felt sympathy for those who weren't Anglicans. Folklore has it that a descendant of Sir James Caldwell, Sir John, was travelling home one day when he chanced upon a Franciscan priest celebrating Mass under a hedge. The weather was cold, wet and stormy and the people were horrified. They had not expected to meet anyone out and about in such foul conditions. They had been caught red-handed. Sir John, a 'staunch Protestant', could have reported them to the authorities, had them arrested, tried and severely punished. There was a long silence after which Sir John took action. He ordered his cattle to be driven out of a nearby barn and told the priest and his followers to take shelter out of the wind and rain and continue their service in peace.

Sir John died in 1744. He requested that nobody apart from his own labourers be present at his burial and that each one be given a guinea. (That was a considerable amount of money at the time.) He also asked that, if they decided to bury him in the family vault, they make sure no rats got in and not put him near his Aunt Jane Johnston.

Castle Caldwell passed to the Bloomfield family when Frances, a descendant of Sir John Caldwell, married John Bloomfield in 1817. His son, John Caldwell Bloomfield, inherited his father's estate in 1849. He was a caring man who realised his tenants had been badly affected by the Great Famine. Many of them did not have enough money to pay rent. He was an amateur geologist who ordered a geological survey of the land. To his great delight he discovered it contained a rich supply of minerals. He could provide jobs by setting up a pottery, Belleek Pottery.

An agreement was reached with two other men, the London architect Robert Williams Armstrong, who designed, built and managed the pottery, and a successful businessman from Dublin, David McBirney, who financed the pottery.

Belleek Pottery began by producing ordinary domestic products. Robert Armstrong realised the local clay was special. It could be used to make a thin, iridescent porcelain, the Parian porcelain for which the factory is famous. They began making small amounts in 1863. This turned out to be a very successful venture. By 1865 they were supplying goods to the United States of America, India and Australia, as well to the nobility, including Queen Victoria and the Prince of Wales.

Robert Armstrong devoted his life to building up the business until David McBirney died in 1882. The agreement between the two men was a gentleman's agreement, cemented on friendship and a handshake. It was not legally binding. David McBirney's heirs refused to honour the agreement so Robert Armstrong lost his life's work. He died shortly afterwards in 1884. Local folklore holds that he loved Belleek Pottery and died of a broken heart. His ghost, a sad solitary figure, haunts the upper storey of the old building.

27

THE DOGS IN
BIG DOG FOREST

*I am grateful to the Fermanagh Tourist Information Centre
for giving me this story.*

King Lir, the god of the sea, was a member of the Tuatha Dé Danann, the ancient gods who lived in Ireland in the distant past. They were huge giants who never died. If they became ill unto death they went to sleep for a thousand years and were laid out on a beautiful bed in a magic room under the sea until they awoke. If a husband or wife went to sleep for a thousand years the survivor was free to re-marry.

King Lir was married and loved his first wife very dearly. They had four children: Fionnuala, Aedh, Fiachra and Conn. Fiachra and Conn were twins. Unfortunately the twins' birth tired their mother beyond endurance and she fell into the deep thousand-year sleep, so King Lir was free to marry again.

It took King Lir a long time to recover from the loss of his wife, but eventually he met Aoife, fell in love and they got married.

Aoife was beautiful but, unbeknown to King Lir, she was an evil witch with a bad, envious heart. She watched her new husband's relationship with his children, became insanely jealous of the love he had for them and decided to get rid of them. She couldn't kill them as they were members of the Tuatha Dé Danann so she wove a wicked spell and turned them into four swans, but that's another story.

Aoife's crime was discovered and as a punishment she was turned into a witch of the air, condemned to live in the eye of a storm, unable to feel anything except pain. Her skin was stripped off and turned into the treasure bag of the Fianna. This went missing and was eventually found by the great Irish giant Finn MacCool.

Finn MacCool was the head of the Fianna and an important person in Irish folklore. His exploits included sorcery, fighting and hunting. He fought great battles and did great deeds, including killing a wicked wizard in Tara, which was the home of the high kings of Ireland. The wizard enraged Finn because he lulled people to sleep by playing sorcerous music, then set the palace on fire. According to folklore, Finn killed the wicked wizard but the other wizards and witches took revenge by bewitching Finn's sister and turning her children, Bran and Skeolan, into Irish wolfhounds.

One day when Finn MacCool was wearing his seven-league boots and hunting throughout the whole of Ireland, accompanied by Bran and Skeolan, who were his favourite dogs, they caught the scent of a witch on the slopes of Slieve Bloom. The dogs had good reason to hate witches, so they chased her. The witch was frightened. She turned herself into a deer so she could run faster. The wolfhounds chased her the length and breadth of Ireland. She began to get tired as they drew near Donegal and the dogs began to catch up with her. She was terrified. She spun round, cast a spell and turned them into stone. Such was their speed that they screeched to a halt forty miles away and have remained there ever since in the form of two small mountains, called Big Dog and Little Dog in Big Dog Forest, County Fermanagh.

28

THE DEFEAT OF LOUGH ERNE'S PAGAN GODS

According to folklore, a monk called Mo Laisse brought soil that had been soaked by the blood of the early Christian martyrs from the Colosseum in Rome and placed it on Devenish Island in the grounds of the monastery he founded there. The ancient remains of his monastery can still be seen today, along with a later, well-preserved round tower.

Mo Laisse was a great scholar and an excellent workman. He took pleasure in copying holy manuscripts, rejoicing in his ability to write in an elegant script and paint illustrations in bright colours and gold. He loved the way sunlight gave the inks on the page a life of their own. He, like the other monks, did most of his work by day until they discovered that the softer glow of candlelight helped in the preparation and painting of gentler colours. It was much easier to work with gold leaf on the rich manuscripts at night because it did not shimmer so blindingly.

Mo Laisse loved his books so much that he worked well into the night, long after the other brothers had fallen asleep. As he worked into the wee small hours of the morning he began to be disturbed by chattering voices.

At first he paid no attention to them, thinking it was simply his imagination or perhaps the lapping of Lough Erne's waters against Devenish Island's rocky beach, which might cause the stones to rattle and the sand to hiss. Mo Laisse comforted himself by remembering that Lough Erne is said to have an island for every day in the year (in fact, it has only 154 islands) and the stones must rattle and hiss on every island. Then, to his horror, he began to hear words, fragments of words, half-forgotten phrases, snatches of conversations. At first he convinced himself it was his imagination playing tricks on him and tried to focus on his faith and his work.

The voices became louder and clearer during the summer months. He found himself straining his ears in an attempt to make sense of them. His work suffered. The pigments he mixed did not have their usual even consistency and his lettering was no longer as even. He was upset by the deteriorating standard of his output and began to wonder if he was being attacked by evil powers. Was he turning into one of those poor pathetic monks who are so touched by the hand of God they become mad? He was terribly worried but didn't want to tell other the monks in case they thought he was crazy.

That winter was freezing cold, with sharp frosts and deep snow. The voices grew louder and clearer and there was no doubt they were talking to him. He recognised the voice of his mother calling. He identified his father's strong, deep voice and, most disturbingly, that of Searc, to whom he had once been betrothed. He remembered asking her to marry him and being delighted when she whispered, 'Yes'. He sighed. Those were happy days, before he had heard the call and taken Holy Orders.

Searc had been furious when he told her of his decision to become a monk. 'You scoundrel,' she had yelled, 'you have ruined my reputation and brought disgrace to my family. I hate you! I curse you and your like.'

She drowned herself in Lough Erne on the day he joined the monks on Devenish Island.

Mo Laisse realised he was listening to ghosts of his past the moment he heard Searc's voice and he knew the only way to get rid of a ghost is to face it. During the shortest night of the year the doors of the other world swing wide open. Creatures living there are able to stride into our world and humans may enter the realm of the Sidhe (pronounced 'shee').

Mo Laisse decided the best thing he could do was talk to the cursed, tormenting voices. He went to the edge of Lough Erne after dark and stood looking across its still waters. The lake looked peaceful in the moonlight. It was difficult to believe demons lurked beneath the dark surface and that all the islands bear traces of their pagan past.

He shivered as he remembered the horror associated with Boa Island, also called 'the Island of the Scald Crow'. It is named after Badb, the Celtic goddess of war, who often took the shape of a crow. During battles she caused the enemy to become confused so her side always won. Battlefields became known as 'The Land of Badb' and Mo Laisse realised he was facing a battle he was unlikely to win. He attempted to calm himself by looking up at the stars. They looked like countless tiny white specks shining high in the heavens.

'I wonder,' he thought, 'if they really are souls of the faithful looking down on earth.'

It was peaceful at first, then he heard the first whispers as midnight approached. At first he thought it was the whisper of the wind through the trees or the hiss of water lapping the shore but the whispers grew louder and louder and, to his horror, he heard his name.

'Mo Laisse … Mo Laisse … Mo Laisse … Mo Laisse … Mo Laisse …'

He recognised hate and fear in the voices.

He stood up straight on the rocky beach and called out, 'Come and face me!' He trembled as his voice was whipped away, shredded by the wind.

'Mo Laisse … Mo Laisse … Mo Laisse …'

The waters shimmered, shivered and shattered as the creatures appeared. They were tall, with wide staring eyes and broad faces that narrowed to a pointed chin. Hundreds glided out of the water and up the beach in a long line.

Mo Laisse was terrified and, almost without thinking, protected himself by making the sign of the cross. The creatures stopped. He now knew they were definitely demons.

'What do you want?' he said, his voice quavering. 'Why do you torment me? I am but a simple man of God.'

The creatures stared in silence, then one moved forward. Mo Laisse caught the scent of death and decaying meat mixed with spices. The creature spoke, 'You have destroyed us!'

'I haven't done anything to harm you.'

'You have destroyed us,' it repeated in a strange accent. It appeared to have difficulty forming the words. 'You have destroyed us. You write words of power that kill us.'

'Don't be silly,' he replied, 'I am a simple monk inscribing the Gospel.'

The creature howled with pain.

'Every colour you lay, every letter you write hurts and destroys us.'

'I don't see how. I mean you no harm. You should leave me alone.'

'We are the last of the Old Ones. You think of us as demons, or devils, but we are neither. Our ancestors lived on this island centuries before Jesus was crucified. We are the last of the proud people belonging to the goddess Danu. Now we are nothing.'

A second figure stepped forward. It was a naked female with large, round, hate-filled eyes. Mo Laisse glanced up at the sky and prayed for the dawn, which would force the horrific creatures to disappear.

The figure said, 'While the people of this land worshipped us we remained strong. Their belief kept us alive and gave us substance. The Sons of Mil arrived with their iron weapons, forcing us to leave this world behind and retreat into the other world. But we still lived in the imaginations of the people and their faith and fear kept us alive. Then Palladius appeared with the first word of the new god. We ignored him. He was old and his word was not widely spread. What harm could an old man and a new religion do to us? We felt we were invincible until Patrick arrived. He was small and dark, yet he yielded a mighty power of terrifying strength. People listened to him. He worked magic and called his magic miracles. He defied the Druids and prevailed! He defeated them in their stronghold, Tara, and we, the gods of Erin, were shown to be ineffectual, weak in our people's eyes. The people of Erin began to turn against us and we began to die, little by little. We were once beautiful. We were known as the Shining Folk. Now look at us! We are hideous.

'You must stop writing that terrible book. Every word you write scars and deforms us. We retreated into the lake long before you brown-robed ones arrived and we could survive if you stopped transcribing that terrible book.'

'Do you mean the Gospel?'

The creature's eyes flashed with rage, 'Yes!' it snarled.

'I can't stop. It is my life's work.'

The female figure gave an evil laugh. 'If something happened to you the work would cease!'

'No, it wouldn't. There would be other monks who would continue it.'

'But they do not have your artistry and skill. Your work is the best in Erin. If you drowned tonight your work would stop for some time, perhaps long enough for us to regain our strength.'

The demon came further up the beach, 'If you won't give us time then we will have to take it ourselves.'

Mo Laisse staggered back and fell on the slippery stones. He thought he was doomed and shrieked in terror. He glanced heavenwards and saw the small thin line of dawn streak the horizon to the east.

'Look!' he shouted. 'You are out of time. God's own pure light is claiming you.'

The demon screamed as it turned to look at the dawn. Its skin began to harden into a solid grey mask. One by one the creatures slid back into Lough Erne's grey depths, all except the female figure. She stayed above the water, her gaze fixed on Mo Laisse, washing him with hate. A grey skin formed on her body, a milky film covered her eyes. She slowly turned into stone as she reached out to touch Mo Laisse. He screamed and wakened the other monks, who found him lying beside a stone idol on the beach. He was sobbing his heart out and babbling incoherently about demons living in the deep waters of Lough Erne.

From that time until the end of his long life, Mo Laisse could not write books. His skill at calligraphy deserted him and he turned to making sculptures. His carvings of saints and other holy men became renowned. After his death, his other work – his dark, bizarre images – were discovered. They were horrific creatures that could only be demons and of these the Sheela-na-gig was the most powerful.

Mo Laisse's carvings remain as a mute testimony of his meeting with the last of the Shining Folk, who lived under the waters of Lough Erne.

Today there is an obscure Protestant sect, called the Dippers, who baptise their followers in Lough Erne because they believe it to be the true River Jordan. They wouldn't do that if they felt the Shining Folk were still lurking beneath the surface of the lake. I wonder if they realise that folklore credits Mo Laisse with destroying the monsters by facing up to them?

29

COUNTRY CURES

In the past there was no National Health Service, doctors were expensive and the majority of the population was so poor so they relied on what we would think of as weeds to cure diseases. Many of these old remedies sound crazy, but scientific research has shown that some of them have a sound basis.

In the past people stored a piece of mouldy bread in a safe place and if they developed septic sores they would wrapped them in mouldy bread. Nobody knew that mouldy bread contains penicillin until Sir Alexander Fleming discovered it in 1928 during the time he worked at St Mary's Hospital in London but they knew that it helped sores heal.

If you suffered from chilblains, the cure was to urinate in a biscuit tin and soak your feet in the tin. It sounds revolting but the liquid in the tin had a high concentration of salts, which drew water, by a process called osmosis, out of the chilblains, reduced the swelling and made feet feel more comfortable.

Cobblers' shops always had spiders' webs festooned in every corner. The reason is simple. It's easy to cut yourself while using sharp knives and working with leather. Bleeding can be stopped by wrapping the wound in cobwebs. The strands of a spider's web are sterile and very fine. When they are applied to cuts they form a net that catches blood cells which helps the wound to form a clot.

There's a folk story about a young lad who was a keen apprentice in a cobbler's shop. His master went out on a message and returned he to find that, in his eagerness to help, his apprentice had given the shop a thorough clean and had disposed of all the cobwebs. 'What do you think you're doing?' The old cobbler yelled. 'Do you want us to bleed to death?'

The 'sensible' old cures, like old traditional stories, were honed over centuries and they do work. They are not as quick acting, strong or efficient as modern medicine but they have fewer side effects. Sometimes today doctors appear to cure one complaint while causing something else to go wrong! Today if I am ill I try a simple folk remedy and if that doesn't work I go to a doctor.

The following list of folk cures is by no means comprehensive. It is just a taster of old remedies that were once commonly used in Fermanagh.

BLACKBERRY

Blackberries produce flowers that vary in colour from white to cerise from May to September. They are common in woods, hedgerows and scrublands and have stems that can grow up to 15 metres in length. They are full of vitamin C, which increases disease resistance. Today we know dark-coloured fruits such as blackberries and blueberries possess chemicals which help prevent cancer.

As well as eating the fruit, the long pliable stems were used to make baskets. It was so useful emigrants took blackberry plants to New Zealand, where whole hillsides quickly became covered in blackberries, which became noxious weeds. Desperate attempts are being made to kill them because they compete too successfully with native plants.

The late Pat Cassidy told me of another, more questionable use of a blackberry stem. He attended school during the late 1920s and there was a boy in his class who hated school. His parents were dead so he lived with a bedridden granny and an old aunt, who suffered from arthritis and was as stiff as a board. One day he decided not to go to school and hid under the bed, thinking his aunt wouldn't be able to reach him. The aunt got a stout black-berry cane and walloped it up and down under the bed. The boy was covered in bruises and scratches and was screaming with pain when he eventually crawled out. He was never unwilling to go to school after that!

Chickweed

Chickweed seeds cannot grow if they are buried deeply so modern cultivation methods have made it less common than it once was. It is a pale green sprawling plant with small white flowers that are produced throughout the year but mainly in spring and summer.

Chickweed is full of vitamin C. In the past, many diets were deficient in vitamin C, so eating chickweed prevented scurvy. It also helps prevent colds and flu. If juice from chickweed is squeezed on boils it'll help them heal.

Whole young raw plants may be picked, washed and used in salads. They taste good mixed with a salad dressing made from lemon juice and olive oil. They also taste good mixed with other vegetables or in a marmite sandwich.

To cook chickweed, boil it in water for about four minutes. Its bulk reduces by approximately two-thirds and makes it taste like spinach. Serve it with herb butters or salt and pepper.

LESSER CELANDINE

(Warning: Do not eat lesser celandine.
It is poisonous, as are buttercups, which look similar.)

Buttercups and lesser celandines
are very similar in that they are
low growing and have cheerful,
bright yellow flowers. Buttercup
petals are rounded while those of
lesser celandine are more pointed.
Buttercup leaves are matt and hairy
while lesser celandine leaves are shiny
and bright green.

Lesser celandines grow to a
height of 20cm. They bloom
from March to May and are
common in damp places.

The common name for lesser
celandines is pilewort because they
were once used to cure piles. People used
to dig up the white bulbous roots, pound them
in a little urine or wine and apply them to piles to
reduce swelling.

CLOVER

There are two types of clover, red and white. It flowers
from May to September and is a sprawling plant that grows in
grassy places to a height of 30cm (1ft).

Clovers have nodules on their roots that fix nitrogen, which acts
as a fertiliser, so it is a very useful plant as it increases soil fertility.

Clover tea helps cure diarrhoea, stomach upsets and chest colds.
The young leaves are edible and can be added to salads, soups and
stews or they can be cooked and eaten like spinach.

According to folklore, St Patrick may have used a clover leaf to describe the Trinity, the three in one – Father, Son and Holy Spirit – because the leaf is divided into three sections. The tradition is that he used a 'shamrock', but nobody knows what a 'shamrock' was. It could have been bird's-foot trefoil, wood sorrel, hop trefoil or clover. Today 'shamrocks' are young clovers, picked before the white curved line on the leaves has developed.

COLTSFOOT

At first sight coltsfoot flowers, which are 10-15cm in height, look like dandelions, but they are borne by scaly, solid stems while dandelion stems are smooth, shiny, hollow and leak a milky substance that was thought to feed lambs. Dandelion flowers are surrounded by leaves while coltsfoot flowers appear during the winter months of January and February before the plant has leaves. Once the leaves appear they have the same shape as a print left by a colt's foot. At first they are small but they grow steadily during the season. In the past they were washed, crushed and applied to skin inflammations and rheumatic joints to cure them. The young flowers were collected before they opened and used mainly in herbal teas to cure bronchitis, laryngitis, coughs, asthma and catarrh.

DANDELIONS

Dandelions are common and grow to a height of 35cm (15in). Their main flowering period is between May and September, but it is possible to find them in bloom during mild weather at any time the year. They have a diuretic effect on the kidneys, causing them to pass more urine than usual. This action helps to wash infections and stones out of the kidneys and the urinary tracts. Their common name is 'pee-the-beds'. When I was a child I was frightened to step on a dandelion, even with my shoes on, in case I wet my bed.

In the past people either boiled the roots to make a tea or simply boiled the whole plant, roots and all, then drank the liquid. The young leaves are delicious in a salad, either on their own or mixed with other salad leaves. They may be cooked like spinach and either served plain or with herb butter, sliced onion, lemon juice and spices.

During the Second World War people washed dandelion roots, cut them into pieces and placed in a slow oven. They were roasted and turned frequently until they became a rusty brown colour after which they were ground and used as a substitute for coffee.

DOG ROSE

Dog roses have flowers that vary in colour from white to deep pink and appear during June and July. The bright red fruits appear in the autumn. Their sprawling stems can grow up to 3m (9ft) and they are found in scrub, woods and hedgerows.

Rose hips are full of vitamin C and are easily turned into a syrup. Split the fruit open, remove the seeds and discard them. Boil the remainder with sugar in water. It is important to remove the seeds because they are an irritant. Children called them 'itchy coos', collected them and considered it a joke to stick them down the necks of their friends' jumpers.

During the Second World War, Northern Ireland's health service gave rose-hip syrup to mothers for their babies and small children. It is sweet so the recipients tended to love it.

Rose hips were also infused to make a tea that was used to cure colds.

ELDER

There are two kinds of elder. They look similar, but one is poisonous and the other edible, so it is important to be able to tell them apart. Luckily this is easily done, despite them having similar leaves and flowers, because the edible elder is a small tree while ground elder grows along the ground. The latter is about 35cm (1ft) in height. It is highly poisonous and should not be eaten. Never use elder flowers unless they are growing on a small tree.

The elder used as a folk cure grows into a small tree about 7m (21ft) in height, with creamy-white flowers that appear during the months of May and June. They are followed by clusters of green fruits that turn from green to red until they ripen and become black.

There is a lot of folklore associated with the elder. It was regarded as the Queen of the Forest, who protected the other herbs. People always asked elder's permission to use it by saying, 'Lady (or Mother) Elder, give me some of your wood and I will give you some of mine when it grows in the forest.' Permission was readily granted but if you didn't ask Mother Elder she turned nasty and got her revenge by bringing bad luck.

Burning elder wood was thought to be very unlucky because the smoke invites bad spirits to come into the house.

Folklore holds that Jesus was crucified on a cross made from an elder tree and since that day the tree has been unable to grow straight.

Babies' cradles were never made from elder wood because it enables fairies to steal the child and leave a changeling in its place.

Elder flowers should be cut after three dry days when the dew has dried but before midday or the flowers will have become slightly withered by the sun. Remove the stems and spread the flowers on racks in an airing cupboard or over a stove. They become brittle within a few days and are then ready for use.

Elderflower tea was used to treat colds and fevers. It should always be made in a china or an earthenware teapot because metal ones spoil the flavour. Warm the pot and place three spoonfuls of either fresh or dried elderflowers for every ½ litre (1 pint) of water. Allow to infuse for a few minutes. Serve and sweeten to taste, preferably with honey, and drink without milk.

Elderflowers can be made into a refreshing cold drink by pouring boiling water on them, allowing them to cool, straining and adding a little sugar, if required.

Elderberries may be turned into a soothing ointment to cure burns. Melt 500g (1lb) of lard in a dish in the oven and use it to cover as many green elderberries as possible. The dish holding the elderberries should be put back into the oven at a low temperature and left for two or three hours, after which more berries should be added and the dish cooked for a further couple of hours. After the second heating, cool the mixture slightly before straining and pouring it into small, warmed jars.

I must say, I prefer the idea of making elderflower ointment to treat burns rather than the alternative old folk cure: covering a burn with fresh cow manure!

To treat spots and other skin blemishes, place elderflowers in a cup and pour boiling water over them. Leave to infuse for several hours, then use the liquid to bathe the skin.

The old folk cures don't have any artificial preservatives so they deteriorate quickly and should be thrown out after a couple of days. It's easy to make fresh batches.

FEVERFEW

Feverfew has light yellow-green leaves and small white daisy-like flowers from May to September. It grows to a height of about 60cm (2ft) and is known locally as mountain daisy. It is easy to grow and it self-seeds on waste ground, hedgerows, walls and in gardens. All the plant parts have a strong smell.

Feverfew has been described as the aspirin of the eighteenth century. It is similar to aspirin in that it affects the size of blood vessels and suppresses inflammation. Medical research has found it keeps the white blood cells, which are always found at the site of an infection, from making substances that damage the body. It has been used to cure rheumatism, arthritis, lumbago, headaches and fevers.

According to folklore, very little feverfew is needed to effect a cure. All that is required is one large leaf, or three small leaves, placed in a sandwich with perhaps a little honey. Eat a feverfew sandwich every day.

GARLIC

Wild garlic is 45-60cm (18-24in) in height. It can be invasive and difficult to eradicate. In spring it develops white flowers and bright green shiny leaves. The garlic genus has won the respect of the medical profession. It used to be widely grown and used in Ireland before the First World War, after which it lost popularity.

Garlic was once used as a cure-all. It was eaten to cure stomach upsets, rubbed on sore, aching joints to treat rheumatism, heated and placed on corns to ease them, squeezed against skin complaints, used as an antiseptic and to cure heart disease. The Greek Dioscorides wrote, 'Garlic doth clear the arteries' thousands of years ago. It would appear that the ancient healers, without any knowledge of the chemical properties of garlic, had somehow stumbled on its ability to help the health of the heart.

Many respectable medical journals have published articles about the effect garlic has on arteries. It has been shown to lower blood cholesterol levels, raise low blood pressure and lower high blood pressure. (It has no effect on blood pressure caused by kidney disease, just the type with the following symptoms: ringing in the ears, dizziness, lack of concentration and hypertension.) It has a strong antibacterial action, so is useful in treating inflammation of any kind and can also be used to treat skin complaints.

During the time I spent working at the Ulster Folk and Transport Museum a beautiful cream-coloured Persian cat called Jason lived in the shop attached to the folk displays. Sally, the shop assistant, took care of him. He was badly troubled by eczema.

His skin condition did not improve in spite of the best veterinary treatment possible. Eventually the vet said, 'There is only one more thing I can try. If this doesn't work I feel the kindest thing you can do is have the poor thing put to sleep.'

Sally was distraught then she thought, 'What's the point in working in a folk museum and knowing about folk cures if I don't try them?'

She bought some garlic capsules, punched a hole in the gelatine 'skin' with a needle and squeezed the garlic juice all over Jason's sores. He looked better by the following day and was completely healed within a short time.

In the past people believed if you hung a clove of garlic around your neck it would keep the devil away!

HERB ROBERT

Herb Robert grows up to a height of 45cm (1ft 6in). It has reddish-violet flowers, which usually grow in pairs at the end of long stalks. The whole plant is very 'hairy', with thick, juicy, forked stems. It is commonly found in hedgerows, woods, stony places and gardens, where it is thought of as a weed. It has been used to treat gout, enteritis and diarrhoea.

To make it into a decoction, to cure sore mouths and tonsillitis, place between one and three teaspoons of dried herb Robert for each cup of water in a non-metal container. Bring slowly to the boil, simmer for about fifteen to twenty minutes, allow to cool and use as quickly as possible. The decoction should not be kept for more than twenty-four hours.

Herb Robert was used to stop bleeding. I once needed dental treatment the day before I went on holiday. Twenty-four hours later my gum was still bleeding. I felt worried and didn't know where to go for help then I saw some herb Robert and thought, 'That's worth a try!' I took some back to where I was staying, washed it carefully and chewed it. The bleeding stopped immediately!

STINGING NETTLES

Stinging nettles are common on the edges of woods, on waste ground, in hedges and in ditches. They produce pale green, inconspicuous flowers between May and September and grow to a height of up to 1.5m (4ft 6in) in height. They have nasty stings that penetrate human skin, causing an unpleasant itchy rash. According to folklore, 'God always puts the urge beside the curse.' Dock plants grow near nettles. They have large, untidy leaves, which, if rubbed hard against a nettle sting, ease the pain, especially if you say the following:

> Docken in, docken out,
> Take the sting of nettle out.

In the past crushed nettle leaves were placed against wounds to stop them bleeding. A gargle made from the juice of nettles was thought to cure a fallen womb, although it's difficult to see how a gargle could help a womb. People suffering from phlegm in the lungs, or who were short of breath, swallowed nettle seeds mixed with honey. Nettle seeds become ripe during the months of July and August.

It was traditional for farm smallholders to eat nettles three times during springtime to 'purify the blood'. They didn't just go out into the fields, find a bed of nettles and start chewing them. Cut 15cm (6in) off the tops, either by wearing gloves or by grasping them firmly (if a nettle is grasped firmly it cannot sting.). Place in boiling water to destroy the sting (a dark liquid will run out of them; it should be discarded).

Nettles were often referred to as 'greens' and are recorded in the following traditional verse.

> Did you ever see colcannon that's made from thickened cream,
> With greens an' scallions blended like a picture in your dream?
> Did you ever take a forkful and dip it in the lake
> Of clover-flavoured butter your mother used to make?

Colcannon is made by mashing warm, cooked potatoes with salt, pepper and a little milk, cream or butter. Then greens are added. These could be scallions (spring onions), cabbage or nettles. The mixture is piled high on plates and a small indentation is made on top and filled with butter. It's delicious!

Nettles can also be used to make tea or soup, cooked like spinach or chopped into a bowl of porridge. They were used by both the Irish and the Scots to make haggis. Nettles were once looked upon as 'wild cabbage'. The plant we recognise today as 'cabbage' is a comparative newcomer in Ireland.

Eating nettles is a sensible thing to do because they are full of iron and vitamin C, so they prevent scurvy, cure anaemia and increase disease resistance. They are the only herb that can be found on the darkest night as well as during daylight hours. The poisonous sting is made from formic acid, which is destroyed during cooking.

Tradition says that once, during Lent, St Columcille decided to mortify himself and his fellow monks by eating nothing but a soup made from nettles. His cook was horrified.

'Can I add anything to the nettles?' he asked.

'No,' replied the saint firmly. 'Only what comes out of the pot stick.'

The cook went away and examined his pot stick carefully. It was the normal, long piece of rounded wood, like a wooden spoon without the spoon attached to the end. It was used for stirring the contents of a cooking pot. He thought carefully about the problem. He didn't dare disobey the saint. He was allowed to make broth out of nettle and 'whatever came out of the pot stick'. Then he had a brainwave. He bored a hole lengthways through his pot stick and was able to run cream, milk, soup stock and other liquids down the hole.

Believe it or not, in the past nettles were used to make a strong cloth that was used for tablecloths and sheets and fishermen used them to make anchor ropes.

PRIMROSE

Primroses grow to a height of 20cm (8in).
Their pale yellow flowers have five petals
and appear during the spring. Their
crinkly green leaves grow in a rosette.
They are endangered in some places
so should not be touched in the
wild. It is possible to buy seeds so
they can be grown in gardens.

In the past infusions of primrose
flowers were used to cure 'bad nerves',
insomnia and headaches. They act as
a mild sedative and candied primroses
make a pretty cake decoration.

VIOLET

Violets, like primroses, are becoming rare, so they should not be
touched in the wild. It is possible to buy plants and seeds to grow
in gardens.

The sweet violet is the violet with the famous scent. It is rare in
Ireland but can be found growing in hedgerows and on the edge of
woods. Dog violets are also found blooming in hedgerows and on
the edge of woods from April to July. Violets grow to a height of
20cm (8in) and vary in colour from blue to white.

Both the leaves and flowers have a high vitamin C content and
taste good in salads. The flowers change colour in the presence of
acids and alkalis, so the acid of fruit salad or lemon juice will make
them go red while cream, which is alkaline, turns them pale green.
They have a slight laxative effect, so it's best not to eat too many!

In the past mothers seemed to be obsessed with the need to cure
their children's worms. It didn't matter if the child lived in the city
and was never in contact with anything that could carry worms.
They had to be cured. My mother used to dose me with senna tea

every Saturday. It tasted horrible and had a horrible effect. I have swapped stories with other people of the same vintage and we all suffered by having our 'worms' treated. Some had castor oil poured down their unwilling throats, some had to take syrup of figs while others suffered the senna tea treatment. The cures differed but the effect was the same. Revolting! I suspect eating violets would have been preferable.

30

THE BELLEEK ONE

*I am indebted to my dear old friend, Declan Forde,
for permission to print his poem 'The Belleek One'.
Declan is a very talented artist, writer and performer with
a talent for making audiences laugh their legs off.*

I was a civil oul' divil from beyond Belleek
Just minding me business and minding me sheep,
I mind me a story I've a mind to recall
Of how three little words can be your downfall.
Me father was civil and I'm civil too –
We're the civillest craturs from here to Belcoo.
Says he as he died, with a glint in his eye,
'When you're stuck for a word son, say, "Aye, surely, aye!"'
I courted a lump from dour Enniskillen
And I hadn't the narve to say 'No' to her bidding,
One night she proposed with a glare in her eye –
Sure I nearly gave in and said, 'Aye, surely, aye!'
I was walking the roads from Belleek to Roslea,
Gatherin' oul' cramery cans on me way
When a quoboy jumped out fornenst Maguire's shed
And throthin' I tell you I thought I was dead:
His face was all black and his clothes were all green
And he whispered into an oul' talking machine,
The pack on his back must have weighed near a ton
And I houl' he shot crows, for he carried a gun.

He mustn't have bin from a neighbourin' townland
For he spoke in a tongue I could not understand;
He muttered and spluttered with his gun in me eye,
So, just to be civil, I says, 'Aye, surely, aye!'
Well, six more jumped out from behind some oul' whins
And they pushed me and pulled me and tied me in chains;
I was trussed up like a turkey and I couldn't have ran
When they bundled me into an oul' transit van –
And me only out getting me oul' cramery cans,
Sure they wouldn't believe me, divil the wan!
They were giggling and laughing and near in hysterics
When their oul' van pulled into the Enniskillen police barracks.
Well, they threw me down in a dark, dingy cell
Surrounded by police and soldiers as well,
Four of them fired me nothing but questions
While two other boyos kept making suggestions.
I paid them no heed as the hours ticked by,
But, just to be civil, I says, 'Aye, surely, aye!'
Well, I'll tell you next day I got the quare shock
As the judge roared at me as I stood in the dock –
'You've made your confession, do you admit or deny?'
Sure, all I could say was, 'Aye, surely, aye!'
I'm not feeling a hundred and I'll tell you the rayson,
I'm lying here now committed for trayson,
For kidnapping Shergar in dead of the night
And riding me Raleigh without any light.
I've admitted committing every crime known to you
And just to be certain, I invented a few.
I'm a supergrass too but what I cannot thole
Is how dare they suggest that I might be a mole!
When I've served all me sentence I'll be two hundred and two,
I'll be too oul' to marry, so what'll I do?
There'll be a rake of new dances and I won't know the steps,
I'll be stuck in the corner and stuck on the shelf.
Boys a boys! I'm a holy tarra', but do ye know what bates the divil?
I wouldn't be here at all at all if I hadn't a bin so civil!

I've made up me mind that starting today
I'll say what I mane and I'll mane what I say –
I'll be civil no more 'til the day that I die –
That's what I'll do, aye, surely, aye!

(Declan Forde, 13 April 1993)

'All I did was say,
"Aye! Surely aye".'

31

FAIRS AND FAKING

Thanks are due to the late Dr Bill Crawford, for giving me the story about the slow sow and for telling me about faking in the first place, and to Brian McMurray and Eddie Carr and to my neighbour, the late Charlie McCourt, who gave me concrete examples of faking in County Down. I am also grateful to Louis Kelly, who originally came from Fermanagh and assured me the practices I described were also common in County Fermanagh. I am also indebted to the late, much-loved storyteller John Campbell for the outrageous tall tale about a splay-footed horse. I don't know where it originated but I can't resist retelling it. All I can say is that it is well known around County Fermanagh because I have heard it on many occasions and I know how much Fermanagh locals enjoyed John Campbell's visits.

An old farmer had a very slow sow. She was so slow she could hardly get up in the morning. In fact, she was good for nothing, so he decided to sell her. He dickeyed her up as much as he could by giving her a bath before he took her to market, but nobody was daft enough to buy her, so he decided to fake her to make her appear less dead and a bit more lively.

The farmer decided to enliven his pig by using a well-known method of 'faking'. He chewed a piece of tobacco then stuck it up her backside! That had the desired effect. She was uncomfortable so she started to move around and looked a bit better, but still nobody bought her and he was obliged to take her home again.

He felt disappointed as he set off, driving the old slow sow in front of him. She was so slow he became frustrated and began shouting. 'Get on, ye baste, ye! Hurry up! Move, ye brute, ye, move!' That had no effect so he started kicking her. She still paid no attention and just kept plodding along very, very slowly. Eventually the old farmer became so annoyed he decided to quicken the slow sow in the time-honoured way by repeating the tobacco treatment. It had a startling effect. The old sow darted off towards the horizon as if she'd been shot from a gun. The only way he could catch her was by sticking a lump of tobacco up his own backside!

Faking was a common procedure in the past. It was a secret trick so it has not been recorded properly. I have been lucky to meet older people, some of whom are now deceased, who were willing to talk to me about it. I was told chewed tobacco, or a piece of ginger, were commonly used to make animals appear livelier. I once met a pair of naughty, elderly twins who laughed heartily when I asked about faking. They said they took a mouthful of turpentine, lifted the animal's tail and blew the turpentine up its backside!

Most of the towns in Fermanagh had fairs where animals, including pigs, were sold. These towns are easily recognisable today because they have a space big enough to hold a large number of people, stalls and animals. They possess either a wide main street or a triangular space, usually called 'the diamond', or a rectangular 'square'. Larger towns had a purpose-built market place, such as the Buttercrane Centre in Enniskillen. It still exists, although it is now a craft centre.

Markets were an important part of the rural economy because in the days when people were self-sufficient ready cash was needed to pay debts. The humble pig was known as 'the gentleman who pays the rent'. A healthy male pig could service a female and the offspring would be shared between the owners of the pair, who would save the money for rent. As a result a pig was looked upon as an important member of the household.

William Carlton, the nineteenth-century author, described the astonishment of a visitor to a small cottage in the early nineteenth century when a pig walked in through the door, climbed up a ladder leading to the half loft and settled down for a snooze. The farmer said, 'That old pig is very clean and wise. It knows when it shares the outshot bed, which is near the fire, to sleep on the side furthest away from the wall. That means if it needs to relieve itself in the middle of the night it can do so without disturbing anyone.

'That pig has sired many fine litters and nobody has a greater right in this house than the gentleman who pays the rent!'

Pigs were easily kept and fed and they could form the basis of a profitable business.

There were several breeds of pigs that are now extinct. The ancient Irish greyhound pig, so called because of its long legs and slim shape, is a prime example and an interesting animal it was too. It was different to modern breeds in that it could jump over fences that were 1.5m (4ft) high. It was intelligent and could be house-trained like a dog and taught to come when it was called. According to folklore, some ancient Irish pigs could, if they lived with a hedge schoolmaster, understand and respond to three languages – English, Latin and Gaelic! (A hedge schoolmaster could be severely punished, along with his pupils, if caught teaching. The only people permitted an education were those belonging to the Anglican Church.)

A house-trained pig was described as an 'educated pig'. It was allowed to wander around all day at will and it returned to the house at mealtimes. The majority of the population were poor so they did not possess much in the way of furniture. They slept on bags of straw and perhaps owned a few 'creepy stools'. (A creepy stool had three legs so it could sit without rocking on an uneven mud floor. Babies learnt to walk or 'creep' by pushing them around, hence the name.)

At mealtimes the potato pot was drained of water and the potatoes placed in a round, shallow basket on top of the pot. The family sat in a circle around the pot and helped themselves. The pig sat beside the youngest child and sometimes squabbled with the youngest members of the family over food.

The large white Ulster was another famous breed of local pig which is now extinct. It gained weight quickly and easily. This was a big advantage because the heavier the pig, the greater the price it would raise when sold. Many large white Ulster pigs became so fat their eyes were covered with rolls of flesh, which caused them to go blind.

Another way of profiting from rearing pigs was to slaughter a large one at home, then take the carcass to market to sell. Farmers put their pork in carts and joined a queue outside the market house to have it weighed. A good market house had a public weighbridge and an honest, reliable operator.

An enquiry into the state of fairs and markets was launched in 1853. It uncovered a lot of dishonesty. Some weighbridges had two sets of weights, one for buying and one for selling. Other weighbridges had slides that allowed a bar to be inserted so the true weight was not given. A farmer with a carcass to sell who did not receive a good price for his pork was on a hiding to nothing. Meat decayed quickly in the days before refrigeration and it was difficult for a family, even a large one, to eat a whole pig before it decayed. Farmers selling live animals, such as pigs, sheep, horses and cows, could simply take them home again if they weren't offered a decent price.

In the 1930s when the Pig Marketing Scheme was introduced. It introduced abattoirs and forbade people from slaughtering pigs

Don't ye worry big boy. By the time I've finished with ye, ye'll look gorgeous!

at home. The large white Ulster became extinct because it had a thin skin which was easily damaged on the way to the abattoir, which reduced its value.

Wealthier farmers' wives salted pork and hung it up in the chimney breast. Pork stored within a dwelling was a sign of wealth, which gave rise to the saying 'bring home the bacon'. When visitors arrived a little bacon would be cut off and shared with the guests, who would sit around talking and 'chewing the fat'.

In Ulster, including Fermanagh, subsistence farming was the norm and ownership of a cow was an important factor in the local economy because it produced manure which was used as fertiliser.

Farmers divided their land into three sections: one for growing grass, one for oats and one for potatoes. The cow ate grass during summer and oats during winter while the farmer ate potatoes and oats. With this system 2 acres of land could feed six people. Manure produced by the cow was so important that dung heaps were kept outside cottage doors to prevent the manure from being stolen! (This was in the days before anyone knew anything about the germ theory of disease.)

The death of the family cow was an economic disaster because a dead cow cannot produce manure, without which the crops failed and the family was faced with starvation. When this happened, farmers were often forced to leave their families and sail to Scotland to earn enough to support his family and buy another cow.

Urine was another important commodity in the past. It was used to tan animal hides. Families used to urinate in the same pot. The urine was taken to the local tannery and sold. If you were so poor you had to sell urine you were 'pisspot poor'. If you didn't even have enough money to buy a pot to urinate in, you 'didn't even have a pot to piss in'.

Urine was used as a mordant when dyeing fabric. (A mordant enables the dye to stick to the cloth.) Families kept a pot behind the house to collect urine for this purpose. Male urine was thought to be stronger and more efficient than female urine. Men were often ordered not to 'waste their urine on the hedge' but to 'put it in the pot behind the house'.

Wealthy farmers with cows to sell who lived at a distance from the marketplace had a problem. Cows that have travelled some way become tired and jaded, which could affect their value. A common practice was to set out after sunset, move the cows to a field near the marketplace, open the gate and drive the cows in to rest and feed. This was called 'stealing the grass'.

Horses were essential to any farmer who had sufficient land to produce a surplus for sale. They were used to plough the land and to take produce to market.

Horses and donkeys for sale arrived at the market place several days before the fair began. Dealers hired gangs of men to take them there. Each man rode bareback on one horse and led about six others strung together by ropes attached to their halters. The men were rough and poorly clad but affable and jolly and they were paid to stay with their charges. They usually slept rough with the animals on the streets. The town centre would be congested by the time the big day arrived and people living in terrace houses could not use their front doors because they were blocked by livestock.

Fermanagh people have a reputation for being hospitable and kind. Women gave refreshments, such as soup, soda falls and cups of tea to men stationed outside their doors.

Buyers strolled around in a nonchalant fashion and tried out stock. The horses stood shoulder to shoulder in a line along the footpath. The chosen animal was raced up and down the road to test its wind, try out its paces and show its shape and prowess. Running horses when there are people around can be dangerous and sometimes individuals were killed, but finding out how a horse moved was important. A good horse will move with the delicacy and precision of a ballet dancer walking in a straight line by placing its back feet accurately in the place just vacated by its front feet. A 'splay-footed' horse makes a mess of drills. How a horse places its feet is absolutely crucial if the animal is intended for use in potato or turnip drills.

The late John Campbell used to tell the following outrageous tall tale about an old farmer called Mickey-Jo and his neighbour, who was a 'hygienic' man.

Mickey-Jo was out ploughing his field when his horse stumbled and fell. The baste picked itself up, gave itself a shake and continued ploughing but it made an awful mess of the drills. It had become splay-footed. The farmer inspected the horse carefully and found the fall had caused it to become cross-eyed. He decided to ask the local vet to come and see what could be done. Before its fall the horse had been a valuable animal and now it was worth nothing because it could not see properly.

The vet came, examined the animal and said he knew how to fix it. It was, according to him, 'no problem'. He went over to his pony and trap and pulled out a length of tubing, which he stuck up the animal's backside before telling Mickey-Jo to keep watching the animal's eyes and tell him when they became straight. He took a deep breath and blew hard down the tube. Mickey watched in amazement as the eyes slowly straightened and the animal became as good as new.

'Right,' said the vet, 'that'll be five guineas.'

'Thon's outrageous!' gasped Mickey-Jo. 'Sure you haven't been here more than five minutes. I'll no give no man no five guineas for a job taking no time at all!'

The vet smiled.

'Mickey-Jo,' he said. 'You're not only paying for my time here. You're paying for my travelling time as well and all the time I spent at university learning what to do. And you're paying for the increase in value resulting from my treatment. That animal's worth thirty guineas as it stands now. Now pay up or I'll put its eyes back the way they were. You know fine well it was in a sorry state when I arrived and you'd have difficulty getting rid of it, unless you wanted to eat it.'

Mickey-Jo paid with great reluctance and hadn't got over the shock of what had happened when the next day the horse stumbled and fell again. Its eyes became crossed and it was splay-footed once again.

'I'm not paying no five guineas to no vet for five minutes' work,' he grumbled as he went to fetch his neighbour, who was an obliging soul.

'When I can
see straight
I'm a lovely
mover.'

Mickey-Jo asked the neighbour to hold the animal's head as he put a tube up its backside. This was a difficult job that took the best part of an hour, but eventually he got it into place, then he blew and he blew and he blew, but the eyes did not move. They stayed stubbornly crossed. 'You've no wind because you're a smoker,' said the neighbour. 'Here, let me have a go.'

It was agreed the two men should swap ends. Mickey-Jo walked round to the horse's head while the neighbour took his place at the rear. The first thing he did was pull the tube out of the horse's backside, turn it round and start inserting it the other way round.

Mickey-Jo was incandescent with rage. 'Why in the name of all that's wonderful did you do that?' he yelled.

'Do you think,' the neighbour replied, 'I'd put anything in my mouth that had been in yours? I'm a hygienic man!'

Horses were a prime subject for faking so buying one was a tricky business. Farmers had to keep their wits about them. Old animals had their grey hairs blackened with Indian ink or they touched up with boot polish.

Fakers inspected lame horses carefully because it took a lot of expertise to make them walk without limping. There were two methods of doing this, depending on the horse. Either the shoe was removed from the good leg or the good leg was kicked hard. Both methods caused the animal to walk evenly.

It's possible to tell a horse's age by looking at its teeth, so some animals had the teeth at the back of their mouths removed to make them appear younger. Sometimes teeth were filed down and a fake black spot placed in the middle of each one for the same reason. Bad-tempered horses were doped to make them appear docile. They changed personality after a few days when the medication wore off. Horses who had pathetic-looking faces with sunken eyes had the hollows injected with water. The water filled the hollows and gave a nice rounded appearance. If a horse had broken wind it was fed ordinary food mixed with lead to hide the defect. Skewbald horses – that is, horses with coats of two colours – were considered unlucky and were often painted. Many a person rode a horse home in the rain to find it changed colour in the process.

There were sometimes shows at markets and fairs. One elderly gentleman I met confessed to taking his prize hens in a large zipped bag on the Larne-Stranraer ferry to Scotland during the 1950s. It was illegal to do so. His wife gave him a lift in their car to a point near the port. She left him there and drove the car onto the ferry so if he got caught there would be no evidence to connect the pair and his car wouldn't be confiscated. All went well until the journey home. He was pleased with himself as he had won many prizes, including best in show.

The ship was delayed by several hours because of bad weather. He began to worry in case his precious prize-winning hens suffocated. He slipped the bag's zip down a bit to allow some fresh air inside. The hens saw the light, thought it was dawn and began to greet it. He was both worried and embarrassed, but all was well. People sitting nearby seemed to think a child had a toy that crowed.

He quickly zipped the bag up again and retired to the gents. The same gentleman confessed to colouring hens' feathers with boot polish while his friend said he kept his hens from crowing by putting elastic bands around their beaks.

Fowl dealers visited markets regularly, bringing birds with them. Some travelled the countryside on bicycles with up to eight half-dead fowl tied to their handlebars. They were usually sold in bundles of five or six with a weakling in among the good ones.

Hiring fairs were held on 1 May and 1 November. Young people made a picnic, packed their belongings in a bundle, which they held proudly under their arms. The size of the bundle was important. A large bundle suggested a thrifty individual, so bundles were often packed with straw to make them bigger, but care had to be taken not to overdo the size. Too large a bundle suggested the owner was either extravagant or an untrustworthy thief! Job hunters stood in traditional places with women along one side of the street and men on the other. They waited patiently for potential employers to come and interview them.

Job-hunting at a hiring fair could be a humiliating experience because potential employers were at liberty to ask personal questions and feel an individual's muscles to find out how strong they were.

Hiring fairs were holidays traditionally, so participants who had found a job were free to go and enjoy themselves, which lent the fairs an air of festivity.

There were many good and generous people who provided good homes for their labourers, but they were hard to find. Anyone with a good job was careful to retain it by giving pleasant, efficient service. As a result many posts were unofficially filled before the hiring fair. Anyone in this happy position simply went to the fair and struck up another agreement with their old boss in the first few minutes, then had the rest of the day off. An individual who had been hired was given a small amount of money, usually a silver shilling, to seal the deal. He or she was entitled to free board and lodging until the next hiring fair when the wage, minus the shilling, became due. Bad employers attempted to annoy their labourers to such an extent that they left and did not have to be paid.

There was a high level of unemployment, so many miserable individuals had to hang around for hours, receiving unreasonable offers from miserly people. Such employers were bad to their labourers, giving them small, unappetising meals and not providing proper beds, so they had to sleep in barns along with the cattle. In these circumstances it was difficult not to become covered in lice.

My grandfather said he was lucky to be an apprentice joiner at an undertaker's in Larne. He was paid sixpence a week and allowed to sleep in a coffin, as long as he didn't soil the interior! He said coffins were comfortable as they were well padded and draught-proof. In cold weather it was possible to slide the lid up so the interior became nice and cosy. 'Many a person,' he said, 'was more comfortable after death than before!'

32

THE BIRTH OF THE RIVER SHANNON

I would like to say a big thank you to Michael Scott,
a great writer and storyteller, for the following story.

To say that Sinann, mistress of the Tuatha Dé Danann, was annoyed is putting it mildly. She was furious.

'I'll get my revenge,' she muttered quietly. 'They've ignored me all my life. Here I am, a member of the Tuatha Dé Danann, but you wouldn't think it from the way they treat me like dirt. They ignore everything I say. They're rude to me. They say I look odd. They don't appreciate my beauty because I'm slightly smaller than them and my features aren't as delicate.

'Nobody wants me. Nobody loves me. I'm all alone.

'It's not my fault I've clurichaun blood flowing in my veins. I'm an outcast among my own royal people and I'm much too tall to be accepted as a member of the wee folk. It's not fair of them to make me an outcast because of an accident of birth.

'I know what those Druid clowns have decided to do ... I can read their minds like a book ... They are frightened of the new race of people who have arrived in Ireland, who possess iron ... The Druids must be powerless when faced with the new weapons ... They intend to preserve their wisdom in the trees surrounding the pool of sacred water before leaving the world of men and disappearing for all time ... They are going to retreat into the secret places of the other world … They'll be hidden in the land below the waves, deep in hidden valleys and on floating island and … they intend to leave me behind.

'They're cowards. They should stand their ground. Stand and fight.

'They should at least search the ancient texts to see if they can discover anything that will combat the power of the invaders.'

Sinann watched the Druids sourly as they approached the seven tall slender trees that surrounded the magic pool. They looked like hazel trees but their leaves were smaller and lighter in colour. Their golden bark and bronze leaves glimmered in the late evening sun. They had an autumnal beauty as they silently dropped their golden leaves into the shimmering water below.

Sinann listened carefully. An eerie silence had settled on the forest.

'That's strange,' she thought. 'I don't hear a single bird singing or even the hum of a bee … I wonder why … Are they afraid of the power locked in the trees … or are they simply showing respect for ancient wisdom?'

The Druids stood in a circle around the pool of dark water. One by one they bowed towards the pool before stepping back and leaving the ancient, most venerable Druid standing alone. The ancient glanced round to make sure he was isolated before bowing to the water and plunging the tip of his long alder staff deep into its dark, glassy, skin-like surface. It caused perfect circles to form across the surface. They widened as they travelled while green and golden light sparkled beneath the depths. One by one the Druids bowed to the circle of trees before retreating to the small animal tract leading to the holy place. The air appeared to grow quieter, softer and gentler as they disappeared out of sight.

When the last of the Druids had left the circle the leaves of plants growing round the pool sprang to life, twisting, turning, moving, growing, blocking the entrance to the grove. Tall grasses, thorns and gorse appeared, forming an impenetrable barrier around the pool.

There was a long silence during which nothing moved. Sinann stepped out from her hiding place. A smile formed on her thin lips. For the first time in her life she felt happy. This was her moment, hers and hers alone. She had been planning it for weeks, ever since the rumour arose that the Tuatha Dé Danann, the ancient residents of Erin, had decided to leave because of the invasion by the Sons of Mil.

When earthquakes had forced the Tuatha Dé Danann to abandon Dé Danann Isle, their original home in the Atlantic Ocean, they had packed their scripts of ancient knowledge into silver ships. As a result, when they arrived in Erin they had knowledge of their old high magic, along with more mundane knowledge, such as how to raise cattle and crops. Their medicines could cure ills and ensure everlasting youth. They had music and knowledge of how to work precious metals, but they didn't know how to defend themselves against iron. The slightest cut killed them, stole their magic power and weakened them, so rather than face the Sons of Mil in battle the Tuatha Dé Danann had decided to abandon Erin.

Sinann stood silently listening. A heavy silence had fallen over the ancient forest. Then she heard it. Far in the distance conch shells sounded in triumph as the Druids emerged from the forest. They were signalling that they had successfully completed their dangerous task.

Sinann walked quietly round the glade, examining each of the seven trees in turn. Each tree represented a branch of knowledge. Together they formed the Seven Schools of Wisdom developed by the People of the Goddess Danu. Within their depths they held the magic mysteries of the ancient world and the secrets of the sovereignty of the Tuatha Dé Danann.

When the leaders of the Tuatha Dé Danann realised they had to leave Erin they decided to leave their ancient knowledge behind to benefit future generations. Deep in the heart of the ancient woodlands they inserted their knowledge into the seven hazel trees surrounding the pool. When the trees matured they would drop their nuts into the water, where they would stay until the sons of men had developed the necessary skills and wisdom to enter the forest and penetrate its defences.

Sinann smiled and waited patiently.

'When I swallow a nut the Druid's magic will seep through my veins. It's mine by right. I'm a Druid too, although the others refuse to recognise me and they continually degrade me. They should have shared their knowledge willingly with me. They are unthinking bullies.'

The trees began to bloom as Sinann watched and waited. Catkins appeared like golden threads and pollen floated from them, filling the air with a golden haze. Nuts began to form. Buds developed, twisting and turning until they formed leaves. The nuts began to swell. They became darker and hardened, then dropped one by one into the dark, silent waters of the pool. Their entrance was marked by a single ripple that shivered across the surface.

The first nuts to fall were out of Sinann's reach, then with increasing excitement she saw one growing near her. It was a beauty. The branch bent beneath its weight and the nut fell. Sinann's long-fingered, slender hand shot out to catch it. She missed but managed to grab it as it entered the water. Her hand plunged in its icy depths up to her wrist. The water felt strange and she found it difficult to bring her hand out into the still air. She smiled as she looked at the golden nut.

'This is my nut,' she breathed. 'The knowledge of the Tuatha Dé Danann will be mine. That was easy. I'll have my revenge.'

She looked up as a terrible thought struck her. Had the Druids put guardians around the pool? Or in the pool? She shuddered and frowned as she looked at the silver droplets of water falling from her fingers. Had anything changed? Had the silence become deeper, almost palpable? Was the air before her eyes shimmering? Was it trembling? Was it her imagination?

Suddenly the pool's water erupted, forming a silver column that swayed towards her. Sinann screamed, turned and ran southward. As she ran she wove this way and that and dropped spells in an attempt to stop the monster, but these had no effect. The monster was much more powerful than anything she had ever known. She raced through the entangled briars and thorns. She thought of attempting to reach one of the blessed spots that offer protection from magic, but even as that thought formed in her mind she discarded it. The water monster had ignored her spells so the blessed places wouldn't help. If she reached the sea she would be safe. The spirit world cannot bear salt.

Sinann ran until her heart felt it would burst and her muscles ached with the effort. She would have reached the sea if she hadn't looked back. What she saw horrified her – a huge, towering figure made of liquid and shaped like a man. It had eyes of fire and sharp crystal teeth shone in its open mouth. She faltered and stumbled. The demon howled in triumph as it fell on her. The monstrous shape dissolved as the water cut a swathe through the earth, swamping fertile fields and drowning villages before entering the mighty Atlantic Ocean.

Sinann screamed and struggled as the water consumed her spirit and absorbed it into itself. She became the river. The knowledge of the Tuatha Dé Danann that she had wanted so desperately became hers as it was absorbed along with her body into the river. The Pool of Knowledge which had given birth to the river fed her and she was nourished by the golden fruits of the Seven Hazel Trees of Knowledge, but she couldn't use it.

The Tuatha Dé Danann heard her screams, wondered what had happened and visited the river. They recognised her voice in the lapping waves, felt magical power surging through its waters and named the river after her, the woman whose anger and greed had been her undoing.

The Celts believed that all wisdom came from water. They immersed babies in water so they would absorb wisdom. St Patrick adapted that ancient belief and made it part of Christianity so today babies are christened by having water placed on their heads.

33

DEATH AND
FUNERAL CUSTOMS

*I am indebted to the late Dr Bill Crawford, John Reihill and
Kate Orr for information about Fermanagh funeral customs.*

People once believed that a sneeze caused the soul to fly out of the
body for an instant. During that short period, the soul was vulnerable because it could be captured by the devil. People said, 'Bless
you', when somebody sneezed to keep the devil from grabbing the
body's soul.

Death, which is the permanent separation of the soul from the
body, was regarded as a serious business, so many precautions
were taken to protect the vulnerable spirit, which was thought to
be on the loose until it found its way to heaven. People thought
souls could become disorientated, get lost and turn into ghosts.
They thought a good soul looks for ways to get out of the house,
so it is free to go to heaven. It was believed that the soul could get
lost if it got confused by a mirror, so once a person died all mirrors
were turned so the reflective surface faced the wall. This kept the
soul from wasting time trying to enter the mirror rather than
going out the window. All windows were opened to make it easy
for the soul to exit.

It was thought important to let the neighbours know of the
death. Good neighbours would know anyway, but, just in case,
the blinds, shutters or curtains were closed, leaving the interior of

the house in darkness. Satan is a creature of the dark, so candles were lit to scare him away.

If you owned a beehive it was important to inform the bees. Somebody was sent to have a conversation with the hive and to cover it with a black cloth.

It was also important to display the body to its best advantage. The body was washed, dressed in its best nightwear and placed on the best bed in the house. Good housewives kept a set of bed linen permanently ready for use in case one of the house's inmates was unfortunate enough to die. If you weren't sufficiently rich to have a spare set of bed linen neighbours would lend you some.

Irish people are famed for their hospitality. There are many folk tales about weary travellers who were lost and, attracted by a light, called at a house late at night, whereupon they were made welcome, fed and given a bed, but when they awoke the next day, they found they had been sleeping with a corpse! I doubt if those tales are true considering the other precautions that were thought necessary to keep the devil at bay when there was a corpse in the house. Four candles were lit around the bed, one at each side of the bedhead and one at each side of the foot of the bed. If the corpse was a Roman Catholic the hands were folded and a rosary was placed in them.

In spite of all the above precautions the devil could still be loitering around the house, waiting to pounce when the soul left the body and nobody could tell when that would happen. It was thought necessary to fool him into thinking nothing was wrong. It was for this reason that people held a wake. A wake was a party that lasted for approximately a week. The idea was that if the devil saw people enjoying themselves, he wouldn't guess that anyone had died. A second benefit was that in the past death was difficult to diagnose, so this allowed more time so people could be certain the person was dead. If a corpse woke up during the festivities, there was obviously no need to bury it! In the past, 25 per cent of bodies moved inside their coffins. The percentage would doubtless have been higher without the existence of wakes.

Men and women performed different functions at traditional wakes. Women kept the men's strength up by supplying a constant flow of food and alcohol. The men's job was to take part in the festivities by eating, drinking and making merry by playing games. Sometimes they played cards, but they were more likely to play physical games such as seeing who could lift a traditional wooden chair in the air using one hand. This required considerable strength because traditional chairs were solid, heavy articles of furniture.

Games of dexterity such as 'Catch the Herring' were also common. In this game a strong stick, such as the shaft of a brush, was laid on the backs of two chairs placed some distance apart. The player sat balanced on the stick with his feet underneath and attempted to pass a small object, which he held in his hand, under the stick, without losing his balance. Very few men could do that. They usually fell off, much to the amusement of the others.

William Carleton described several wake games, including 'Horns the Painter'. The players sat in a circle on the floor while the leader sat on a chair, or stool, in the centre. The leader said something like, 'Horns, horns, goat horns', while holding two fingers up to the centre of his forehead to indicate horns. He spoke very quickly and the others were expected to follow his actions. If he mentioned an animal that did not have horns and any player indicated horns that player suffered a penalty, such as receiving a slap.

Once the wake had ended the body needed to be placed in a coffin and buried. The owners of small, overcrowded houses that did not have any beds kept the corpse in a coffin stored under the table. Some houses had narrow tables especially designed to hold a coffin (they were the same length and width).

Traditionally the coffin was carried from the house to the cemetery. Four men linked arms and balanced the coffin on their shoulders. All the men, apart from the old and infirm, took it in turns to give it 'a lift'. After the invention of the motor car the coffin was usually carried along the road to the end of the farm, then it was slid into the hearse and brought to church for the funeral ceremony. Mourners walked in a solemn procession behind the coffin. Traditionally it was only men who followed the coffin and attended the interment. Women were allowed to go to the church service but some stayed away to prepare a meal for the men when they returned after the funeral service and interment. Once the men had been fed the women could have something to eat.

In the past people who went into a coma were thought to be dead and were buried before they recovered. The most famous example of this is not found in County Fermanagh but in County Armagh. In Shankill churchyard, Lurgan, there is a gravestone dedicated to 'Marjorie McCall 1705, lived one, buried twice'.

Marjorie was married to a doctor until she 'died' of a fever. Fevers were contagious so she was buried quickly, wearing an expensive ring. Nobody could remove it because her fingers were so badly swollen. Grave robbers heard about the ring, dug her up, opened the newly buried coffin and attempted to remove the ring. It was stuck firmly on her finger, so they decided to saw it off. They fetched a saw and set to work. Marjorie woke up the minute she started to bleed. The robbers got such a shock they fled the scene. She climbed out of the grave, went home and knocked three times on the door. Her husband was drinking with the family, bemoaning her loss. He turned to his children and said, 'I could swear that was your mother's knock.' When he opened the door he got such a shock from seeing his wife standing there, in her shroud, he dropped dead. He was buried in the grave she had vacated. Marjorie lived for a long time after her first burial. She got married again and had several children with her second husband.

In the seventeenth century, grave robbers who stole goods from graves but left the body behind were common. The eighteenth and early nineteenth centuries saw the rise of a new kind of grave robber: the body snatchers, also known as 'resurrection men' and 'sack-'em-ups'. Medical science was in its infancy and doctors were keen to learn about how the body was constructed. Stealing corpses and selling them to medical schools or for anatomy lectures and demonstrations was a profitable business. Naturally relatives objected so measures were taken to foil the sack-'em-ups. Corpse houses were built in graveyards. They were of a fairly standard pattern, roughly 15x20ft (about 4x6m). Coffins containing the newly dead were placed inside and guarded by well-armed friends and relatives. Large numbers of guards were needed to act as a deterrent because the sack-'em-ups weren't fussy about whether you were alive or dead when they snatched a body. The guards stayed with the body for several weeks until it was thought to be sufficiently decayed to be of no further use.

There was a bizarre trade in hair and teeth as well as bodies. The hair was made into wigs and teeth were stolen for people who had lost theirs. A folk tale records the sad story of a girl who bought teeth because she wanted to look good on her wedding day. The teeth stolen from a corpse were stuck into her gums, which became infected, resulting in her death. The following verses describe the sorrow of a corpse on having its hair and teeth stolen.

> As for my hair – the auburn hair
> You used to love so well;
> Alas, it's gone to deck the head
> Of lovely Mrs. B.

> And when my skull came back from St-rk,
> That clever organ-finder;
> It was found out that Cr-owo-r
> Had plucked out every grinder.

The idea of having somebody else's teeth stuck into your gums is enough to make any person living today shake with horror, but many tales of transplants have been preserved in folklore. The great Ulster giant Finn MacCool is said to have had been given a skin graft from a sheep because he suffered a large flesh wound. The graft was so successful he had to have the wool sheared every year.

According to the late Tom McDevitte, there was a group of sack-'em-ups quietly digging up a grave by the Anglican church in Lisnaskea. At the same time, a couple of young local boys had raided an orchard. They wanted somewhere quiet to divide their spoils. They didn't know there was a group of sack-'em-ups working in the graveyard as the men were digging with wooden spades, which are quieter than metal spades. The boys thought nobody could hear them and they began to count aloud. 'One for you and one for me. One for you and one for me. One for you and one for me.' As they neared the end of the division some of the apples dropped and rolled away. One of the lads turned to the other and said, 'You keep the rest and I'll run down and get those big ones that have rolled near the gate!' The sack-'em-ups fled, convinced the devil was claiming souls and was after them!

(The Anatomy Act was passed in Westminster in 1832, making it illegal to dissect a body in Britain and Ireland without a proper death certificate and the heyday of sack-'em-ups came to an end.)

34

PHIL PURCELL, THE PIG DROVER

This is one of my favourite stories. I love telling it.
Originally I got it from William Carleton's book
Traits and Stories of the Irish Peasantry.

Phil Purcell had a long, lean, solemn-looking kind of a face. In spite of his sober appearance there was something amusing about him. He made people laugh, even though he was a real rogue.

Phil was interested in pigs, particularly the greyhound pig. It was an ancient breed of pig that has since become extinct. It was called a greyhound pig because it could run fast, had a slender body like a greyhound and long legs. It was an intelligent animal and could be trained like a dog. (Before dogs came to Ireland pigs filled the role of man's best friend.)

Phil never liked dogs much. He preferred pigs. They provided him with a living. He didn't have any land of his own but bred pigs by teaching them to forage for themselves along road verges and in woods. He was often seen walking around the roads with a clatter of pigs behind him.

During his travels Phil often met strangers who had travelled. He developed an urge to see a bit of the world himself, but he was poor. He needed a cunning plan. After a lot of thought he decided to sell a couple of his less intelligent pigs to scrape together the fare for the Liverpool boat, so he could sail across to England.

He would train a group pigs as champion escapologists by teaching them to jump over fences, return to him and walk some distance behind him. He reckoned he could sail to Liverpool with a herd of pigs and sell them. The pigs would escape, find him, then he would travel by night and move on to another village where he could sell them again. It was a perfect plan. Nobody would look twice at a lone stranger dandering along the road at night and there would be no reason for anyone to suspect he was accompanied by a herd of pigs!

Phil put his plan into action and soon, with the help of his favourite pig, had a squad of healthy piglets. He started training them and was delighted to find they'd inherited the intelligence of their father. In no time at all they were ready for their big adventure.

The cheapest way to travel was to stay with the animals so Phil boarded the Liverpool boat and cuddled up with his pigs on the lower deck. He was very happy. He preferred the company of pigs to that of humans. They were not argumentative. They did what they were told and they were affectionate, good company.

Once they had landed Phil started to walk away from the city with the pigs following at a discrete distance. He was tempted to sell his pigs at Liverpool market but thought better of it. With all the hustle and bustle of dense traffic it would be difficult for them to pick up his scent. They could get lost, separated from each other, travel in different directions and be gone for good.

As he walked along the road Phil admired the scenery. The countryside was flatter than at home and the grass wasn't as deep a green in colour. He was surprised to find all the women wearing long dresses. At home ladies had short dresses and bare feet. He missed the sight of shapely ankles. Eventually he found a farm up a short lane. It was tidy.

'There's a man with a wheen a money,' he thought. 'And he's got a couple of pigs fenced in beside the house. That fence will keep his big fat animals in but it'd be no trouble at all for my boys. Bless those poor pigs. It doesn't look as if they ever get into the house. Doesn't yer man realise pigs are clever animals and there's nothing like an educated pig sitting beside the fire to keep you company?'

Phil saw the farmer working nearby, went over to him and asked if he'd like to buy a couple of pigs.

The farmer looked critically at Phil's pigs.

'They're very thin.' he commented.

'Aye, they are. They're Irish pigs. They're half starved, the craters. Don't you know there's a famine in Ireland? Sure isn't that why I've brought them over here. I want to give them a chance at a better life. Examine them carefully. You'll see they're healthy. You'd be able to fatten them in no time at all and make a wheen of a profit when you sell them,' said Phil, lying through his teeth. He knew fine well it was impossible to fatten a greyhound pig.

The farmer examined Phil's pigs. They had bright eyes. They were lively and showed no signs of disease, so he bought two. Phil was pleased, said his farewells, dandered a couple of miles along the road and sat down under a tree to wait. He felt warm and pleased with himself so he had a bite to eat and a doze. His remaining pigs foraged nearby. Now to see if the next part of his plan worked. Sure enough, after dark his pigs appeared. Phil praised and petted them and gave them a treat – a turnip he'd 'found' in a field. He gathered his herd together and set off, walking briskly along the roads. He'd covered ten miles by the light of the moon before he found a place to lie down and sleep.

Next day Phil sold all his pigs, including his favourite. It was the last to go. He was offered good money for it and it seemed a shame not to make the most of the opportunity. That pig was an exceptional pig. Phil loved it and worried in case it was housed in a barn with no possibility of escape. He was so anxious he couldn't even doze and determined that if his pet pig didn't manage to come back he'd go and steal it. That would be a risky procedure, but he loved that pig and didn't want to part with it. He was heartily relieved when it was the first to return. He greeted it with open arms and sat cuddling it until the others came back.

Each day Phil sold pigs and each night the majority managed to come back to him. He did lose an occasional pig, but he reckoned that was par for the course. He was happy. He had more money than he'd ever had in the whole of his life, he was accompanied by his

'Of course I look smug.
I'm a well-educated greyhound pig.'

beloved pigs and he was seeing new places. Life was good; however, several weeks later, when he was drinking quietly in a pub and enjoying a bit of *craic* with the locals he heard there was a scoundrel abroad selling pigs. The law was after him and when he was caught he could be tried and hanged. In those days there were newspapers, but few people could read them. Telephones, radio and television didn't exist so news travelled slowly; nevertheless, Phil decided discretion was the better part of valour so he sold all his pigs, except his favourite, and headed for the Liverpool boat.

He knew the peelers were following close behind and he had to get away as quickly as possible or risk arrest but when Phil reached the Liverpool boat his heart rose up into his mouth in horror. The captain was refusing to sail because the boat was overcrowded. He demanded that half the people get off or the boat would sink when it reached open waters.

Phil stood beside his favourite pig and thought and thought and thought. Then he had a brainwave, an idea so brilliant his sober face creased into a smile. He approached the captain and said, 'If I solve your problem by getting half the people off your ship, will you grant free passage for me and my pig?'

The captain agreed and said not only would he be granted free passage but he, and his pig, could sail with the other passengers rather than travelling with the animals.

Phil borrowed a megaphone, climbed halfway up the stairs to the bridge and shouted, 'Will all the men from Monaghan throw all those from Cavan off the ship?'

He knew there was a lot of bad feeling between those living in the two counties. Mayhem ensued. Bones were broken, skulls cracked, people were killed and in no time at all approximately half the people were either off the boat, so injured they couldn't object to being carried off or dead and their bodies were simply thrown overboard. The captain was delighted and set sail immediately. As they left the dock Phil watched the peelers arrive and breathed a sigh of relief before settling down with his pig to enjoy the most luxurious and enjoyable voyage of his life.

35

THE LADY
OF THE LAKE

The beautiful daughter of a wealthy landlord lived in a mansion near Enniskillen. She was known to have the gift of second sight and people came from miles around to have their fortunes told as whatever she foretold came to pass.

When she was 19 years of age she foretold he own demise, saying that she would die before her twenty-first birthday because of a man's jealousy.

One night, when she was going home after visiting a friend, she was stopped by a local farmer. He had asked her to marry him, but she didn't like him and had refused the offer.

Again the farmer asked her to marry him and she refused. The man was drunk and he fell into a drunken rage.

'I suppose you think you're too good for me!' he raged, as he started to beat her. 'Well, if I can't have you nobody can.'

The poor girl was beaten so severely she had to be taken to the local hospital. There she managed to whisper, 'Bury my body on Devenish Island and be careful because taking my coffin across to the island could be dangerous.'

After she died, a boat carrying the girl's coffin, accompanied by a large number of mourners, was being rowed across the lake when a storm moved in. The boat was pitched from side to side. The coffin sank from sight under the turbulent lough waters and all the mourners were drowned. From that day to this it is said that the ghost of the beautiful young woman may be seen gliding over the shimmering waters of Lough Erne. Few people will dare to be anywhere around Lough Erne near Derryhinch after dark.

Some years ago a party of anglers were fishing in the district. It's a pretty place and the lake is famous for its pike and perch. They heard the story of the Lady of the Lake.

'That's a lot of nonsense,' laughed one of their number. 'I don't believe in ghosts. They're just a figment of people's imaginations.' He made a bet with his friends that he could camp on the lake bank alone for a night.

Next morning when his friends came to find how he had got on, they found he was so shaken by the night's events he could hardly speak. Eventually he managed to tell them that during the night he had seen several people carry what looked like a coffin onto a large boat, which was filled with people, mainly women. It set off from the Derryhinch shore and he watched until it was about halfway across to Devenish Island, at which point one of the figures in the boat stood up. The boat rocked from side to side. People screamed, then there was a splash as the boat and its occupants disappeared in a flash of light.

It has been said that the ghostly figure of the young girl has also been seen flitting from island to island and around the tombstones surrounding the sixth-century abbey that stands on Devenish Island, but there is no need to be frightened. She was a gentle girl. Her ghost does no harm. It brings good luck.

36

FOLK TALES ASSOCIATED WITH MARBLE ARCH CAVES

*Thanks are due to Richard Watson, who has worked in
Marble Arch Caves for a long time, for the following stories.*

Marble Arch Caves are the longest known cave system in Northern
Ireland. They take their name from the nearby Marble Arch, which
is a natural limestone arch at the upstream end of Cladagh Glen,
under which the Cladagh River flows. They are near the village
of Florencecourt.

In the past the arch over the river was used as a roadway for
people living on Cuilcagh Mountain. A young local girl called
Maggie Duffy was running down from the mountain and across
the arch when she fell through the hole and into the river below.
She was wearing wide, voluminous skirts, which opened like a
parachute so she floated downwards and lived to tell the tale.

In 1912 a group of German tourists, who had been mountain-
eering, walked along the banks of the Cladagh River and were
startled to see an elephant walk towards them and start drinking from the river. There was nobody around and the Germans
were puzzled. They did not think elephants lived in Ireland.
They retired to the nearest pub and asked the bartender.

He responded, with a straight face, 'That's right. You're likely to spot an elephant drinking the Cladagh waters. You weren't hallucinating. There's a simple explanation. There once was a wealthy landlord who lived locally. He was a great traveller and brought elephants to Ireland from India. He sold his estate and went to live in England, leaving his elephants behind. They seem perfectly happy here. They eat the local vegetation, drink the river water and when the weather turns cold they move into Marble Arch Caves.'

What the bartender failed to say was that Duffy's circus made regular visits to Fermanagh. They kept elephants and they were giving local performances at the time.

That seems an appropriate way to end a book that started with Fermanagh tall tales!

GLOSSARY

ANOTHER CLEAN SHIRT'LL DO YE	you won't live much longer
AULD	old
BAD CESS	sewage which is not breaking down by normal chemical process into nitrates and water but stays foul smelling
BASTE	beast
BLITHERING	stupid
CEILI	a sociable gathering during which people swap stories, sing, make music and possibly dance
CHANGELING	a fairy left to replace a stolen human
CLART	an untidy, careless person
CLURICHAUN	a type of fairy that resembles a leprechaun. According to the poet, W.B. Yeats, clurichauns are rare and tend to imbibe too much alcohol. They can be found in rich men's cellars
CONSUMPTION	tuberculosis
COT	a type of boat found only in County Fermanagh, which is preserved by being sunk under water
CRAIC	chat, fun

CRATUR	a pet, as in 'the poor creatur' or a drink, as in 'wud ye like a wee drop of the cratur'
DANDERING	ambling in a relaxed fashion
DICKEYED UP	dressed up, made to look as attractive as possible
DON'T FEEL SO HOT	not feeling well
EEJIT	fool
EYES OUT ON STALKS	look astonished
FEAR GORTA	man of hunger
FELLA	fellow
FUTTERING	fiddling with something
FAKING	to make something look much better and of greater value than it is
GEIS	a very serious oath that must be honoured
GIRNED	complained
GOMERAL	stupid person
GOSSOON	young boy
GUB	mouth
HAET	heat
HAULT	hold
HERPLING	walking as fast as possible with a limp or some other difficulty
HOITY-TOITY	stuck up
HOKING	poking around looking for something
HUNGRY GRASS	a grass-covered space where someone has died of hunger. It is difficult to get off hungry grass and staying on it leads to death
INTIL	until

KEENING	a type of mournful singing performed by women at wakes. Banshees may sometimes be heard keening when warning of death. A crowd of keening banshees is said to warn of the death of an important person or of war. Folklore holds that crowds of banshees were seen and heard singing before the outbreak of the Second World War
KNOCK THE MELT OUTTA	fight with fists
KYRIE ELIESON	Lord have mercy
LARN	learn
LAUGH YER LEG OFF	a hearty laugh
LIKE A DOSE OF SALTS	the salts are Epsom salts, which cause severe diarrhoea
MO LAISSE	Saint Molaise
SODA FARL	a type of flat bread which is baked on a griddle. The raising agent is baking soda, which works in conjunction with an acid, usually buttermilk
PALLADIUS	a monk who brought Christianity to Ireland before St Patrick, the patron saint of Ireland
PEELERS	policemen
REDD UP	tidy up
SCULLERY	a room that served as a kitchen
SHINING FOLK	members of the Sidhe
SIDHE	fairy folk
SONS OF MIL	an early race of people who inhabited Ireland
SOUTERRAIN	an underground cave

STEPPING OUT	the beginning of a serious relationship that could lead to marriage
STILLER	an individual involved in the distillation of poteen
TARA	where the high kings of Ireland were crowned
TARGE	bad-tempered woman who is always scolding
THON	yon
TITTER OF WIT	wise up
TUATHA DÉ DANAAN	ancient gods of Ireland
WEAN	child, literally 'wee one'
WEE BITE	something to eat
WEE CUP OF TEA IN YER HAND	refreshments taken beside the fire, or in any other informal setting, without laying a table
WHEEDLING	to cajole someone to do something
WHEEN	a lot of
YER MAN	any man who is the subject of conversation

BIBLIOGRAPHY

Bannon, Edel, Louise McLaughlin and Cecilia Flanaghan, *Boho Heritage: A Treasure Trove of History and Folk Lore* (Fermanagh: Boho Heritage Organisation, 2009).

Bell, Sam Hanna, *Erin's Orange Lily: Ulster Customs and Folklore* (London: Dobson Books, 1956).

Cunningham, John B., *The Great Silence: The Famine in Fermanagh 1845-1850* (Belleek, Fermanagh: Davog Press, 2012).

Drumskinney: Memories of Rural Life in North Fermanagh, As told by local people (Fermanagh: Drumskinney Rural Action Group, 2009).

Glassie, Henry, *Irish Folk History, Tales from the North* (Dublin: The O'Brien Press, 1982).

Glassie, Henry, *Passing the Time: Folklore and History of an Ulster Community* (Dublin: The O'Brien Press, 1982).

Glassie, Henry (ed.), *The Penguin Book of Irish Folk Tales* (London: Penguin Books, 1985).

Herbert, Vicky, *Lisnaskea Workhouse, Past, Present and Hopefully Future* (Belleek, Fermanagh: Davog Press, 2010).

Kinealy, Christine, and Trevor Parkhill (eds), *The Famine in Ulster* (Belfast: Ulster Historical Foundation, 1997).

McCusker, Breege and Frances Morris, *Fermanagh: Land of Lake and Legend* (Donaghadee, Down: Cottage Press, 1999).

McGuffin, John, *In Praise of Poteen* (Belfast: Appletree Press, 1988).

McVeigh, Jim (ed.) Joe McVeigh, *In Ederney Long Ago: Stories from the Ederney District 1939-40* (Manorhamilton, Laois: Drumlin Publications, 2000).

Mercier, Vivian, *The Irish Comic Tradition* (Oxford: Clarendon Press, 1962).

Morash, Chris (ed.), *The Hungry Voice: Poetry of the Irish Famine* (Dublin: Irish Academic Press, 1989).

Morton, Robin, collated works of John Maguire, *Come Day, Go Day, God Send Sunday: The songs and life story, told in his own words, of John Maguire, traditional singer and farmer from Co. Fermanagh* (London: Routledge & Kegan Paul, 1973).

Murphy, Michael J., *Ulster Folk of Field and Fireside* (Dundalk, Louth: Dundalgan Press, 1983).

O'Súilleabháin, Seán, *Irish Wake Amusements* (Cork: Mercier Press, 1967), translated from the original Irish *Caitheamh Aimsire ar Thórraimh* by An Clóchomhar in 1961.

O'Sullivan, Patrick, *Irish Superstitions and Legends of Animals and Birds* (Cork: Mercier Press, 1991).

Reihill, John James, *Friday's Child: 70 Years of Island Life* (private publication).

Reihill, John James, *Hands Across the Sea: The Life and Times of Annie McManus Reihill* (published by John Reihill, 2003).

Reihill, John James, *Reflections of an Islander* (first published by John Reihill, with the financial support of Aughakillymaude WEA History Group, the Fermanagh Trust and the Local History Trust fund, 1996; reprinted in 2001).

Rogers, Mary, *Prospect of Erne* (Fermanagh: Fermanagh Field Club, 1967).

Scott, Michael, *Irish Animal Tales* (Cork: Mercier Press, 1989).

Scott, Michael, *The River Gods* (Bray, Wicklow: Real Ireland Design, 1991).

Trimble, Dianne and Cunningham, John (eds), *The Fermanagh Miscellany 2011* (Enniskillen, Fermanagh: Fermanagh Authors' Association, 2011).

Trimble, Dianne and Cunningham, John, (eds), *The Fermanagh Miscellany 2013: The G8 International Edition* (Enniskillen, Fermanagh: Fermanagh Authors' Association, 2013).

Wilde, Lady, *Quaint Irish Customs and Superstitions* (Cork: Mercer Press, 1988).

Wilde, Oscar, *The Happy Prince and Other Stories* (London: Bodley Head, 1960).